Also By B.G. Vandenberg

The Immortal Coil Saga

The Gate
The Mage Crown

For Jennifer, Jackie, and Kim

CONTENTS

1

OOPS!... I DID IT AGAIN

Octavia

The rain is cold today.

I've got my layers on, but they don't keep the chill from reaching my bones as a car speeds past, pulling me out of my frozen thoughts and dousing me with water from a puddle on the road.

"What the actual hell!"

I wipe the water from my face, tucking the blonde, wavy strands behind my ear, and look up at the sky – solid gray to the horizon. I smile as I scan the low-hanging clouds, ripe with more downpours. It's a welcome sight, and while there's plenty of time to get to the grocery store and back home before the skies clear, that isn't the real challenge.

Seth got in late from Houston last night and practically fell asleep before his head hit the pillow. His trips exhaust him, and I expect he'll sleep late, so going now means more time with him when he's up. I don't want to miss a second. The hard part will be making it back home before he wakes up and finds me gone. I would have made this trip earlier in the week, but the unusually sunny weather made it dangerous, especially without him at home.

My forearm itches, and I scratch it absently, still pissed I got soaked. My fingernails pull at the skin from a blister, my heart skipping a beat when I feel the warmth of blood. I slap my palm over the little wound and press hard. Feet frozen in place, my eyes dart from one side of the street to the other. Less than a block away, a figure stands outside the store beneath the damp awning. My heartbeat thunders in my chest as my breath catches; the long rain slicker, galoshes, and umbrella are a dead giveaway. I feel a trickle slip from underneath my hand, watching as the figure makes a slow turn in my direction.

Idiot!

All the breath leaves my body at once. I made a ridiculous and deadly mistake assuming I'd be safe, and I'm *anything* but safe right now.

I consider running, my legs trembling as I rock back on my heels. Screaming will only draw more attention, and I certainly don't want that because, despite my best effort, I've just been scented by a vampire. Sure, it's raining, but they aren't wild animals. The rain burns them, but umbrellas and rain gear cancels out that risk. And besides, what dumbass would risk becoming dinner?

Me.

Stay inside, Tavi, Seth warns me every time he leaves, though it's more like he's begging me. And what do I do? I tempt fate and do stupid things like this. Stupid because I am walking gold with my A negative blood.

My stalker's steps quicken as he closes the gap between us, and I feel so stupidly helpless. I mean, I *am* powerless, but I don't have to act like it. One deep breath in, and I spin on my heel and sprint down the sidewalk.

Maybe I can deter him if I can find a long, wide puddle.

I eye what looks like a tiny lake and veer right for it, but before I can splash through, tires squeal before me. I scramble to a stop inches before swan-diving across the hood of a white Mustang.

"Tavi!" Seth flings the passenger door open, *the look* marring his face.

Well, shit.

I'm in trouble.

Seth hits the accelerator before I get the door closed. I twist around and watch the vampire slow, then stop in the middle of the street as we speed away. I slide back around and buckle my seatbelt.

Several minutes pass in relative silence – the roar of Seth's Mustang and the wet slap of the wipers keeping the tension alive. I slink down in my seat for no reason except to avoid eye contact with my boyfriend. Not that he's even looking. His eyes are fixed on the road, the muscles in his jaw clenching. It's not raining anymore, but I see several red blisters where he must have gotten wet getting out of the house to the car. He opens his mouth to take a breath, and I see the two tiny bulges under his upper lip receding.

I'll never get used to seeing that.

A little shiver runs down my spine. Vampires kill people like me, but he's not a vampire in my eyes. He's just my boyfriend, Seth.

"How bad is it?" His quiet tone is forced, his knuckles white against the wheel.

I lift my arm and show him the new, fresh scab and dried blood. He glances at it and looks back at the road. "They can smell it–"

"A mile away. I know."

We drive past a cheerful sign proclaiming *Safe Travels! Come back and see us soon!* and I know exactly where we are headed. My stomach lurches, and I stifle a sudden wave of nausea. "Do we really need to see Illion? It's only a scratch."

"We'll go to the cabin first. I need to make some calls." He grabs my hand and squeezes it. "You can clean up your arm, but yes, we need to see Illion."

"I know." I'm pouting, primarily for effect, but the nausea doesn't subside, and now it's joined by dizziness. As a human, walking into a vampire's lab feels like volunteering for something exceptionally unsavory. But, like it or not, he's the only reason I'm not a human blood bag and actually have a life to live. The night Seth saved me from his brother would have been for nothing if Illion hadn't broken every rule in the book to conceal me.

We wind through the pine trees on a back country road without saying a word, and I steal a quick glance at Seth. His brown eyes are a storm, worried and angry at the same time. It's not lost on me that, for his whole life, he risked everything just to exist, then doubled down by being with me. Seth left his lavish life as a rising son of the Dormande family to hole up in a backwater East Texas town with me. He did it all to keep me safe from his own kind because I am not supposed to be free.

The story I've heard my whole life was that my parents had done the impossible by keeping me hidden from the collectors since I was born. The midwife, paid handsomely to report me as a stillborn, swapped my records with another baby who actually *had* died during childbirth which falsely classified me as type B blood. Apparently it worked perfectly with my parents genotypes.

From then on, I was the most protected child ever. My parents homeschooled me. I never wore shorts or skirts or rode a bike. No sports. No sewing. Absolutely nothing that carried the risk of drawing blood. They raised me to understand that even the tiniest scratch was a death sentence, one we could take no chances with.

Now, here I am living with a vampire. I shake my head as I watch the trees lining the road. *Oh, the irony.*

Seth pulls onto the dirt driveway leading to one of two secluded hideaways he's procured. We alternate between them when I need Illion's services. He has arrangements with a few locals to come and clean after we leave–insurance no vampire will catch wind of me or follow us.

Trudging inside the little cabin, I drop my tiny purse on the bed, peeling my shirt off as I head for the bathroom. But before I reach the sink, Seth is behind me, my hair fluttering from his speed, wrapping his arm around my waist and pulling me in close.

"Why do you scare me like that?" he mumbles as he nuzzles my neck, sending little shivers across my scalp. I lean back into him, the tension in my shoulders finally coming undone.

"Keeping you on your toes?"

"Lame," he chuckles, resting his chin on my shoulder where I can see him in the mirror. His smile fades, and his expression goes dark again. "Seriously, Tavi, you know you can't just go out. My father and his people are everywhere."

"Why don't we just find a fae commune and live there? No one ever sees them. They are practically invisible." I twist around to face him, lifting my arms over his shoulders and playing with his soft brown curls, which is hard to do, given his six-foot-four stature.

"We don't hide with the fae because they are weirdo hermits that detest outsiders. Especially my kind."

I lean my forehead on his chest and breathe deeply, enjoying his strange scent—it's not a cologne or even the fine-grained sand he uses to bathe. I can't compare it to anything because it's just *him*. Besides, the only other man I've been near for any length of time was my father, and he *definitely* didn't smell like this. Maybe it's a vampire thing.

"You know, you're really hot when you get angry," I murmur, sliding one hand down to toy with the dragon pendant hanging from his neck.

"Oh," he smirks, "I'm not angry." He lifts me and, with unnatural speed, we are in the bedroom where he sets me on the bed. "You want angry?"

My heart flutters, and heat rises from my core.

God, he's good.

I give him my best damsel in distress face, though my thoughts are definitely not damsel-like.

"Are we safe for now? Or do we have time for you to get really," I hook my fingers in his belt loops and pull him toward me, "*really* mad?"

He collapses over me, our lips finding each other with more restraint than I thought possible. Gently nipping at my bottom lip, his attention moves to my neck, his stubble brushing the soft skin below my ear. My hands are still in his hair, my nails running along his scalp. One of his hands slides down my side, following the curve of my ribs to the top of my hip, goosebumps erupting in its wake.

His kisses are maddeningly delicate, teasing me with anticipation as my body begs for more. He hovers above me, placing his lips on my chest, just over my heart.

"If I knew a near-miss would get me this kind of treatment, I'd do it more often," I murmur, arching against him.

He pauses, his entire body tense, then rolls to the side and props himself up on one elbow.

"That's what I'm afraid of." He sighs, resting his free hand on my stomach. His palm traces a circle around my belly button, carefully avoiding the four medical ports on my abdomen. Then he lets his fingers trail down the thin, jagged hysterectomy scar beneath the waistband of my jeans. "You have to be more careful, Tavi."

The way his hair falls across one eye... *Damn*. Combine the shadows from his cheekbones with the perk of his upper lip? I marvel at what has to be the most beautiful boy in the world.

"I'm sorry." I grasp his hand with both of mine. "I know I can't just wander around like that." I grin, unable to help myself. "I just really wanted some Oreos."

He groans with a smile, a moment of brightness before his face goes dark. He tightens his fingers around mine and pulls our hands to his lips before he tucks them against his chest. "I'm being serious. I can't stand watching you suffer during Illion's treatments."

Just the mere mention of what awaits is enough to silence me. Illion claims to have figured out a process to mask my blood type, albeit in the most agonizing way possible. The ports he placed in my abdomen irritate me, but they are a small mercy, so I don't have the additional pain of so many needle sticks every time I require treatment.

"I know. I'll do better," I promise. "I just wish you didn't have to leave all the time. It gets creepy when I'm in the house alone."

"When you're without me, or when you are low on snacks?"

"Both," I smirk.

"Sweet pea," he leans down and plants a kiss on my forehead, "I'll see to it we never run out."

Seth's Texas drawl is slight, but when it surfaces, my heartbeat quickens, and I'm sunk. I don't know how I can fall even harder for him, but I do with every word and every touch. I pull him down for one more kiss, desperate to get lost in him. He obliges, then pulls us both up and gives me a playful push toward the bathroom.

"Get that arm as clean as you can. We need to be out of here in ten minutes; I already texted Ben and Amelia to come and clear this place."

I make it to the sink and look over my shoulder before I finish cleaning up. Seth is looking down at his phone, pacing; all the cool and collected confidence is gone. He's worried and nervous and he's trying his best to hide it from me. I memorize his expression and file it away in my brain under "this is why you don't do stupid things, Tavi."

I love him too much and it's time I started acting like it.

2

HOLD YOUR BREATH

Seth

TAVI STANDS AT THE sink, and I can't help but watch her. Shirt still off, she's in a sports bra, giving the mirror an opportunity to flash glimpses of the ports on her soft belly. My hands twitch with the desire to cover them, to make them disappear. She catches me staring and smiles, but I can see the fear lurking in her eyes.

When we first met, I wouldn't have been able to be near her if she bled. It didn't matter if her blood is poison to me. Most blood isn't, and unfortunately, I can't tell the difference by sight or smell. The control I have now has been years in the making.

It's a tricky thing, cleaning a bloody wound, but she's had practice–*too much practice*–and it's not fair. As she finishes up, I catch her gaze in the mirror again. This time I smile, though inside my guts are turning in on themselves.

We walk a razor's edge, keeping her hidden, and every time she exposes herself, we inch closer and closer to discovery, which scares the shit out of me. I want her to have a life, a life with me, but not at the expense of her safety.

"Time to go," I call as I open the front door.

Within ten minutes, we are in the car and winding through the pine trees. I glance at her out of the corner of my eye, trying to gauge how she's doing by the look on her face. She has always been hard to read, but there's no mistaking the fear that creeps into her ice-green eyes whenever Illion is involved. My fingers flex against the wheel, the leather resisting despite my strength. Illion's lab is only twenty miles down the road, so we are coasting onto the gravel drive before I see the telltale sign of her nerves.

"How soon before you have to go back?"

I tighten my grip on the steering wheel. She tries to distract herself with small talk—always her go-to—but I don't know what to say. My answer will only make it worse.

Finally, we pull off the road and coast down the long drive to Illion's place. On the outside, it is just a simple country house, but it conceals an extensive underground laboratory complex he uses for his questionable research.

"Dammit, Illion," I whisper to myself when I notice the garage door isn't open. I texted him before we left the safe house. He knows this needs to be quick, and he knows I can't risk anyone seeing us here. That's when I notice the tire tracks in the grass beside the driveway, and a pit forms in my stomach.

"What?" Tavi follows my eyes, but she doesn't see what I see.

Illion's not alone.

The door beside the garage cracks open just wide enough for me to see Illion in the shadows. The way he's standing, like he's about to run, tells me everything I need to know. It takes a lot to set a vampire on edge, and he's sending his message loud and clear. I take a slow breath and focus.

As casually as I can, I ease out of the car, beckoning for her to crawl out on my side. If Tavi knows something serious is at play, she'll panic. She looks like she's about to repeat herself as she climbs out, but I go completely still and hold my finger to my lips and she halts mid-exit.

Please don't panic.

Thankfully, we've been together long enough for her to know when to do exactly as I say, and I count my lucky stars we work together like clockwork. I point to the car door, miming my intention to slam it closed. Then I point to the ramshackle garage.

Go, I mouth, nodding towards the door where Illion is barely visible in the recessed shadows. I need her to make a break for it. I suck in a deep breath, my muscles pulling taut against my bones. Masking her footsteps is critical. There are others somewhere on the property, and the only way I can be found here is if I'm alone. She can't see what I'm hearing, but she trusts me. The rusted door cracks open a little more so Tavi can see it, a familiar skeletal hand beckoning from the shadows. I scan the area as I pull my leather jacket on, then I give her the signal.

One.

I mouth the word and lock eyes with her.

Two.

She gathers herself like a cat about to pounce.

Three.

She bails, launching herself toward the entrance, turning sideways and disappearing into the shadows just as I slam my car door shut. The garage door closes. The driveway is dangerously still. It all happens in the space of a breath.

I don't even have a chance to take another one before leaves rustle on the side of the building. Bending down, I pretend to inspect my front tire as two figures glide out of the shadows. They are whispering words I cannot hear to one another, but they stop once they step into the light. One of them paces around to the back while the other approaches me. I'm a little surprised at their audacity.

"Greetings."

I look over my shoulder and act surprised, pretending I've been startled.

"Think I ran over a nail." I sigh, dropping my head and trying to appear exasperated. "Pulled in here to make sure I wasn't going to blow out on the highway. Illion is a friend."

The woman steps closer. "We spotted you as you headed out of town. You were in quite a hurry."

"Nah," I laugh and stand. "This baby's a Mustang. You're not really driving one unless you're hauling ass."

I grin, leaning back on my car and crossing my arms, trying not to wince as the water from the hood seeps through my jeans. My left hand casually reaches up to scratch my collarbone, but instead pulls my jacket collar to the side, just enough to reveal the dragon's head pendant hanging around my neck. The silver-embossed shape flashes in the late afternoon sun breaking through the retreating clouds. "Now, how can I help you?"

The female takes a step back at the sight of my pendant. *As she should*. But the male, finishing at the back end of the car, walks closer to examine it.

Unbelievable. He must be new.

I frown and shake my head. The man's eyes flick up to my face, then to his partner. Their eyes meet, and she takes another step back.

"Our apologies, Mr. Dormande."

"An apology doesn't cut it," I growl. "Stalking me would not go over well with my mother."

"Why aren't you in Hou-" the man starts, but the woman shushes him with a quick slice of her hand.

I narrow my eyes. "Did my father ask you to keep tabs on me?" The man's the one I'm addressing, but the woman cuts in.

"We're just making our rounds, sir. We had a few collections in the next county, and we stopped by to pick up some samples on our way back to Houston."

She's a terrible liar. I dismiss her lame response, push off the car, and stand close enough to feel her breath.

"You can go." I purposefully change my tone from bothered to demanding, getting the effect I was hoping for. The pair drop their eyes.

I don't want to leave Octavia alone here with Illion, but I don't have a choice. I need to get these goons as far away from here as I can, and quickly. I tell myself she will be alright, though I know she is terrified.

Fighting every instinct I have, I grit my teeth, open the car door, and slide inside. The motor roars to life as I slam the door, narrowly missing the pair as I back down the gravel road. I pause at the end of the drive and wait to see what they will do, unsurprised when they follow me.

A dark blue sedan eases along the highway's shoulder behind me, but before the car can reach Illion's driveway, I punch the gas and back out in front of them, just missing the bumper by a hair as I yank the wheel and point my car down the road. Pumping the clutch and shifting into gear, the engine revs as I fly down the highway before they can pull back onto the road.

Keeping an eye on my rearview mirror, I strategize. I have to figure out how get back to Illion's undetected before Tavis starts her treatment. There is no way in hell I will leave her to face it alone.

3

THE CHEMICALS BETWEEN US

Octavia

"OH, OCTAVIA. WHAT HAVE you done?"

I flinch and drop my eyes, shame prickling my face. When he speaks to me like that, I feel like a four-year-old in trouble. But my answer *is* as ridiculous as a child's.

"I tried to go to the store."

It sounds even worse when I say it out loud. My chin quivers as I realize how close I have come to being discovered.

"Let us hope your foolish risk hasn't been Seth's undoing."

I turn, ready to protest, but he is halfway down the metal stairway, the light from the crack in the garage door falling on the metal handrails. The speed at which he moves will never *not* unnerve me.

Close the door.

Illion's voice drifts through my mind like a sticky, humid breeze, and I cringe, but I do as I'm told, then hesitantly pick my way to the basement. He has already begun preparations, clinking glassware and rummaging sounds echo from the next room. I scratch my arm nervously, catching myself just before I open the little wound again. Pulling down my sleeves, I suck in a breath and step inside. Shivers run down my back when the disinfectant smell fills my nose. A wave of nausea rises, and I swallow hard to keep the bile down as I eye the familiar procedure chair.

Hurry, Seth. I don't want to do this alone.

Illion weirds me out as much as he frightens me. I watch as he skulks around mumbling to himself. He has two distinct personalities - the introverted scientist and the extroverted jerk. Tonight, he's channeling more of his introverted self, and I'm glad. The jerk was no fun the last time I had to get out of a scrape.

"Octavia," he says, drawing out the 'a' in the middle of my name, "I honestly don't understand why you keep getting yourself into trouble." He flicks the bubbles out of a full syringe. He finally turns toward me, one eyebrow raised. "Are you unhappy being alive *and free*, my dear?"

My cheeks flare. I thought we were being sensitive, but he's not playing the introvert after all. I lean against the the procedure chair. I can't quite bring myself to sit in it yet.

"I am as happy as I will *ever* be." It comes out in a sad whisper, revealing my shame—which also sad and quite depressing.

The older vampire turns his back and sorts through paraphernalia on a metal tray. It's like I haven't even spoken. My inability to stay quiet gets the better of me and I continue.

"I have to hide during beautiful weather. The world is only safe for me when it rains." He turns and levels a hard stare in my direction. I shift in my seat but manage to shrug, trying to play it off. "Haven't you heard of seasonal affective disorder?"

"Oh," he murmurs, "you are a clever one, aren't you?" One second he's by the sink; the next, he's a breath from my face wearing an infuriating smirk. "We all know you are positively thrilled to be... *functional.*" Illion over-enunciates that last word, and I cringe.

I hate it when he's right.

The fact that I can think for myself, break the rules for myself, and even get into trouble for myself is a gift. If it weren't for Seth and Illion, I'd be another blood bag in some vault providing appetizers at a Directorate event. The truth of the matter is, Illion is not a human sympathizer. Given the opportunity, he'd gladly open any of my veins and bleed me dry. A vision of him with a maniacal smile and a blood-filled wine glass flashes in my head, and

I shudder. However, his loyalty is to Seth, not the Directorate - for what unlikely reason, I still don't know.

And their tenuous relationship makes me extra nervous to be in his lab alone. One bite, one slice, and it's over for me. Illion wouldn't draw any ire from the Directorate. In fact, he'd be celebrated–he allegiance to Seth be damned.

I drop my gaze to the floor, chewing on my lip because there's nothing else to say. It would be super helpful if Seth showed up now. On top of the panic-laden anxiety I already feel, the greenish glow of the lights in here and the awkward silence are nerve-wracking. Things are getting *very* uncomfortable.

Illion smirks and then returns to his tray of supplies.

"Your bravado is commendable, Octavia." He lowers his voice. "But you still need to work on controlling your heartbeat. You sound like a squirrel."

Sometimes, it's hard to tell if Illion despises me or takes pity on me. His tone is strained, probably because he must exert enormous willpower to keep from attacking me without Seth here to intervene. He's never been so bold, but I imagine he wouldn't hesitate if the stakes were lower.

"Was it the Directorate? Outside?"

Jesus, I'm so brave, it makes me stupid. I never ask questions, but without Seth here to keep me in check, my nervous chatter is running out of control.

Only the rattling of metal instruments on metal trays and the clanking of glass vials answer my question.

Fuck it.

"Why-"

"You do remember I work for them, don't you?" He doesn't even look up. If I were him, *I'd* probably kill me.

Minutes drag on, and I have just about given up hope when the door creaks open. Brown curls peek around the frame as Seth steps into the room. My feet can't carry me to him fast enough.

"Hey," he breathes at the nape of my neck as I fling myself at him. He smells cool and damp, like the night air. My fingers curl in the hair on the back of his head, and the sharpened edge of my panic immediately dulls. Everything feels safer now.

I pull back and press my forehead to his. "Are you okay?" I ask, my hands sliding down the creaky leather of his jacket.

Our fingers entangle, and I lean into his chest. His heartbeat is steady and slow. Seth releases my hands and cups my face, tilting it upwards as our lips meet in the softest kiss.

"I am now," he whispers.

"That encounter was... unexpected." Illion's disapproving tone breaks my reverie.

Seth wraps his arms around me and squeezes before he brushes past me, pacing around the room. "It took me an hour to be sure they weren't tailing me. I came back on the old Talbot farm road."

"Isn't the bridge washed out?" I cut in.

"Yeah," Seth grimaces. "Mustangs aren't the best off-roaders."

"Enough about your travel log." Illion puts a hand on Seth's shoulder to quell his frantic energy. "Let's get on with it."

Illion turns towards me, the clinical blue-green lights casting shadows on his angular face and making him look more sinister than usual.

"All right, precious. I'm not immune like Seth, so let's get that decadent smell of blood out of the air before I lose my self-control."

I eye the chair for a moment before climbing into it. My hands hover at the bottom hem of my t-shirt, and I hesitate before looking to Seth. He presses his lips together and nods, resting a hand on my thigh.

"Go on," Illion prompts me. His growing irritation is evident in his voice. I swallow hard and tear the fabric over my head, letting it drop to the floor beside me. Seth picks it up, draping it over his shoulder before he begins to buckle the wrist restraints anchored to the chair. I stay quiet.

I did this to myself.

I say to myself so maybe next time, I will remember how much I hate being chemically cleansed before I take another stupid risk.

Seth's hand lingers on mine while Illion hovers over me, attaching a bundle of thin tubes to the four small ports on my abdomen. The elder vampire was smart enough to know I'd need his services more than once, so he put the pearl-sized ports in the first time we met. Now I only have to endure his chemical concoction and not his needles—how very kind of him. He snaps into the last port just under my ribcage and moves away from the chair.

"Can you dim the lights?" Seth's voice is quiet — a warning of the coming pain. I nod and bite my lip, my breaths speeding up to match my racing heartbeat as the lights fade to a comfortable twilight.

"I'm right here, Tavi." I can feel Seth's thumb sliding back and forth on the top of my hand. It's the sensation I focus on when my treatment begins. Four pinpoints of fiery pain blossom into one another until I am wrapped in a blanket of hot coals. All the breath leaves my body as I convulse. My muscles contract, and I'm convinced my bones will break if they tighten anymore. Anyone else would be screaming, and I did the first few times, but I have learned to disconnect from the pain by this point.

Illion's concoction courses through my veins, weaving through capillaries and veins. He told us he designed a specific molecule that binds to the surface of my red blood cells. It masks my blood type and makes me invisible to others of his kind. The drawback is that it doesn't last forever, and my nerve cells react violently to the serum.

Imagine being scrubbed all over with a cheese grater and then doused with lemon juice. Every inch of my body burns. Even my eyeballs.

"I can't..." I pant. *I can't do this anymore.*

"You're okay. You're okay." Seth's voice is right by my ear; a desperate whisper twisted from my pain. As the onslaught of treatment dissipates, I can feel his arm cradling my head, his fingers wrapped in my hair. As the serum is fully released in my bloodstream, I start to shiver from a combination of shock and sympathetic nervous reaction. Also, I'm covered in sweat, and the chill of the room cools my skin like a north winter wind. My stomach churns, and Seth puts his hand on my cheek to help calm the violent shuddering of my jaw. Illion is already pulling the tubes when Seth shifts me forward to drape a blanket around my shoulders.

As hard as I try, I can't keep my stomach from turning somersaults, and I heave. My muscles struggle to respond, weak and rubbery from all the seizing. I can't stop myself from rolling forward, but Seth's arms band around me, keeping me out of the sick and adding what little body heat he has back into my flesh.

"Help her, Illion." The desperation in Seth's voice breaks me. I want to tell him I'm okay, but I'm not. I couldn't speak if I tried.

Cold hands touch my belly, and I feel the click as one of my ports is reattached to a line. Relief floods through me as pain relief and sedation seep into by system from the new line, then everything fades and I am delivered into quiet, agony-free darkness.

4
BAD HABITS

Seth

"WHY ISN'T SHE AWAKE? Did something go wrong?" I pace around Illion's study, burning through my anxious energy. I know I'm hovering, but something is *wrong*. As many times as we've had to do this, I can tell.

Illion glances up from his notes.

"She's perfectly fine."

I never know when the bastard is being sarcastic. I stop pacing and crouch beside Octavia. She doesn't look fine unless pale skin–paler than usual–and strange, labored breathing is normal, which it's not. She's on the suede loveseat in Illion's office, and as I lean over to grab a blanket, something falls from my shoulder. I stare at the thin, blue sweatshirt lying in a heap at my feet. My lips thin. It's another reminder of what Octavia's been through. I don't bother putting it on her.

She's gone completely limp, and I'm afraid I might hurt her. Her hair, still damp from sweat, sticks to her face, so I brush it behind her ear, ignoring the hint of a sting on my fingers. She's been put through the wringer, and most of it is my fault. My job wasn't to fall in love with her, but here we are.

I never meant for it to get like this.

"She isn't fine, Illion. She should be awake." The color red creeps into the edges of my vision as the anger rises inside me, twisting and taking root in my tone. I stiffen and stand as warning thrums in my blood—Illion notices. "What did you do?"

He sighs and sets his instruments down, tilting his head up towards the ceiling. "I can feel your anger all the way over here. Deep breaths, my boy. Don't go nuclear."

"What," my voice drops into a growl. "...did you *do*?"

"I administered a serum I designed *specifically* to keep your little princess safe. There are no clinical trials, Seth. Every dose is a risk. Both of you know that. But she's going to be fine. If she were going to die, it would have already happened."

Closing my eyes, I take in a deep breath to get control of my temper. His answer is not good enough.

I lean down to tuck the blanket under Octavia's chin and smooth her hair back. Illion is still sitting by the treatment table, sorting through tubes and glass vials, and nearly falls backward off his rolling stool when I appear beside him, crossing the room in a blink of an eye. He takes a moment to recover, tugging the sleeves of his jacket up higher on his forearms, and stands. My jaw ticks as I lift my chin. I forget how tall he is.

"Spare me the theatrics, son. We all learn to move like that as toddlers." He takes the tray to the counter, then strides into his office, pulling a decanter and two glasses from his bookcase. The liquid inside is a rich honey color. He raises a glass in my direction. "Bourbon?"

I shake my head.

Illion pours a glass for me anyway and sets it on the little table in front of the loveseat, easing into a worn wing-back chair near his desk.

"Since I've established Octavia's death isn't imminent, can we relax?

I ease onto the loveseat beside her and tuck her feet onto my lap, ignoring the glass of bourbon. His behavior is different tonight. As long as I've known him, I've never fully trusted him. Tonight, that trust has dwindled even more.

I start with the obvious. "Why was the Directorate here?"

"Why wouldn't they be?" Illion huffs out a chuckle and knocks his bourbon back in one swallow. "I work for your father, or have you forgotten the predicament you've placed me in? They were picking up samples when you called. I got them out of here as fast as I could."

Fair point.

Illion is one of my father's top scientists and his personal sanguine sommelier. His skills at detecting and refining blood are unparalleled, making him an invaluable asset to the Directorate, specifically to my father. In fact, he was the cornerstone of the Dormande's rise to prominence thirty years ago. As New Orleans, the whole of Louisiana, and the rest of the Deep south, were solidly under the control of the Vincents, Arthur Dormande took a risk and established himself in Houston. Not so far from New Orleans that he was without resources, but far enough that he could tighten his fledgling grip. Not surprising that a place like Texas had resisted control, but Arthur approached the region like a businessman, not a tyrant. Illion shared his vision and played an integral role in the Dormande takeover of the region.

Illion pours another bourbon, examining it in the low light. "How long have we been at this?"

The hair on my neck rises. We've had this conversation before.

"Three years."

"How much longer are you willing to run this..." his eyes finally find mine, "marathon?"

"Hyperbole much, Illion?" I snatch the glass of bourbon because I'm going to need it if we're going down this road.

"My boy, I've watched you and Octavia the entire time you've been together. It is clear this has become something bigger than you or your mother thought it would." He takes a thoughtful sip from his glass, then rolls the crystal back and forth between his fingers. Squinting, he catches my eye through the amber liquid. "In no iteration does this end with you and Octavia and a happily ever after."

My jaw clenches. Illion can push my buttons almost as quickly and efficiently as my father can.

"Why not?" I take a mouthful of the bourbon and swallow hard. "We can leave."

A slow smile creeps over the elder vampire's face.

"Leave? How could the son–*one of the heirs apparent*–to the Dormande family simply vanish?" He laughs openly, smirking as he takes another sip of bourbon and sets the glass on he table beside him. "Seth, please. You are a very intelligent young man. Can we use our brains here?"

"What if I don't want it?" I finish the glass. The alcohol burns as it warms my belly and inflates my ego. "Eventual leadership of the family empire is not on my list of life goals. Cain can have it; I am more than happy to walk away."

But that's just it. I can't, and I know it. The muscles in my jaw clench and unclench. I knew the risks when I agreed to hide Octavia for my mother. It's just a matter of time before my father and his henchmen catch up to us.

"I'll take her west. The controlling families past the Rockies stand on less tradition. They're more progressive."

Illion cannot hide his amusement. His attempt at suppressing a smile is ineffective.

"There you have it," he chuckles. "Tell me, why haven't you already done that?" He steeples his hands and rests his chin on the tips of his long, skinny fingers. "Is it because you are too deeply ingrained in the fabric of this family? Genevive Dormande could hardly allow her favorite son to spirit away what you helped her steal." He drops his hands and picks up the glass of bourbon, taking a long sip.

"Want it or not, it's yours. Your twin cannot handle the intricacies of managing the Dormande empire. You got the brains. Your brother got something else entirely, whether your father wants to admit it or not." Illion adds the last statement under his breath as he swirls the last of the bourbon before he drains the tumbler, sucks in a sharp breath, and sighs. "You know the truth of that as well as I."

"Cain and I are twins, Illion. We're the same."

"Of course you are. How silly of me." Illion snickers, his eyebrows raising as he glances at Octavia. "Sleeping Beauty stirs."

"Be kind, will you? And if you can't be kind, be quiet," I growl under my breath as I shift and see Octavia's eyes fluttering. She's not quite awake, but will be soon, then I have to convince her to trust me with her life even more than she already does when I take her to Houston–my family's stronghold.

5

IS IT OVER NOW?

Octavia

"How long was I out this time?" I try to speak, but it comes out more like a croak than my voice. Seth helps me sit up and reposition myself to lean against him.

"Three or four hours," Seth whispers near my ear, his arms banded loosely around my waist. Every time we go to Illion for help, it gets more painful and takes longer for me to wake up. *That can't be good.* I lift my head and look at Seth. He gives me a little smile, then pulls me in tighter. "Don't worry."

"She should worry."

I flinch. Illion has such a way with words - and impeccable timing.

"Not now, man," Seth warns. "She's just waking up. Give her a minute."

"I am making a fair point." Illion shifts his position in the armchair across from us. "As I said not five minutes ago, these treatments are experimental. We don't know what the long-term effects will be." He crosses his legs and rests his arms loosely on the arms of his chair. "I don't even know if they will continue to be effective, which begs the question," he looks down his nose at me, "why do you keep tempting fate, Octavia?"

I close my eyes and curl into Seth's side because I know Illion's right. If I had stuck to the rules Seth and I agreed on, I would never have had to endure these treatments and put all of us at risk. I don't know why I can't control my need to take chances. Seth's fingers track soothingly up and down my arm. Maybe a childhood of protection bordering on mania has something to do with it. But if I want to stay with Seth and keep living, I have to get myself in check. I clear my throat and do the unthinkable.

"Illion," I suck my teeth, bracing myself for what I'm about to say, "you are right. I've been stupid and reckless."

If the situation weren't dire, I'd giggle at the look of surprise on the vampire's face. Even Seth looks confused when I turn to face him. I place my hand on his chest and toy with the pendant he never takes off.

"I've drawn too much attention to us this time. I mean, we're trying to avoid that, not invite it."

Seth sits forward and after a hard kiss to my forehead, stands. I'm still a little woozy, but I join him, and he tugs me along, only releasing my hand to grab his jacket and shrug it on.

"Where are we going?" I ask, but I don't care. Not really. I'm ready to crawl in a hole and stay there if it means I stay safe and with Seth. I'm ready to never have one of these treatments ever again.

"I have an idea."

Seth grabs my hand again and pulls harder, encouraging me to move faster.

"Your father is going to increase his efforts to look for you, you know," Illion calls, still in his chair.

Seth looks over his shoulder and gives Illion a nod, but he has already opened the door and pulled us halfway through it.

"Do take care this time, children," Illion's voice carries through the door, even as it closes.

We slip out of the lab and climb the metal stairs to the ground floor. This time, his car is actually inside the garage, though it's covered in mud from his earlier evasive maneuvers.

I slide into the passenger side, and Seth closes the door gently, still keeping the sound at a minimum. I flinch at the engine's roar, but Seth notices and quickly kisses my temple before he throws the gearshift into reverse.

"We'll be okay, Tavi."

I catch a glimpse of Illion standing in the shadows just before the door completely closes, which sends a shiver down my spine. The car rolls forward and in seconds we are on the road. As the landscape flies past in the fading twilight, Illion's words replay in my mind. *Why do you keep tempting fate?*

"Seth, I'm sorry. I really am." I keep my eyes on my lap, picking at my fingernails. I can't even look at him.

He reaches for my hand, and I am soothed by the familiar way his thumb strokes across my chilled flesh before he gives it a little squeeze. "I told you it'll be fine. I've got a contingency plan."

I can't disguise the quizzical look flashing across my face. "Contingency plan?"

He smirks as he grabs the steering wheel with both hands, and oddly, it puts me at ease because I love that look - I can't help it. A section of his hair has fallen over one eye, and my stomach flips. Even with his chiseled features, there is still something soft and kind about him that defies convention. I take in the view. He really is a beautiful creature, though I catch the faintest clench of the muscles in his jaw. My fascination is tempered with reality because I realize he's trying to maintain his confidence even though he's not convinced. Though I trust him with my life, I'm starting to wonder if he really knows what to do.

"Where are we going?" I wait, but the sound of the tires on the road is the only reply. He's not talking, so I know it has to be something risky.

"This is no bueno.," I murmur under my breath. He would do anything for me, even if it could get him in trouble, or worse. He switches on the turn signal, but not toward home.

Okay, definitely something risky.

"We are going to see my mother. She'll help. She always does."

6

IT'S IN MY BLOOD

Seth

OCTAVIA'S EYES ARE WIDE, staring at me like I've grown another head. I know she thinks I've lost it. I would think I'd lost my mind, too. There is no safe place for her in Houston, especially at my family's residence in the heart of the city. I tear my eyes away from her face and back to the road. Oddly, it's also the safest place, if I'm there with her.

"I know it sounds crazy; I do." I grip the steering wheel harder, twisting the leather until it squeaks.

"Your mother? The woman who feeds on people like me?" Octavia exclaims, leaning closer - so close I can smell her fear." The woman who is married to the fucking Grand Master of the Directorate? *That's* your plan?"

"You don't know her, Tavi. She's not like my father." I frown. I don't want her to see my irritation, but my knuckles go white, making it painfully obvious. She has no idea that her freedom was my mother's idea, not mine. I wish it had been mine, but at that time I was still trying to reconcile the disgust I felt for my family with my unfailing and tragically moral sense of duty.

Helping my mother get Octavia out was a way to seek redemption, nothing more. God, I wish I could explain everything to her, but the less she knows, the better. I doubt she'd understand. "It's going to be awhile. Why don't you get some sleep?"

Octavia's eyes linger on me, searching for an explanation I can't give her. Despite this bomb I've just dropped on her, she hesitates, but then she folds her hands against my shoulder and lets her head fall on top of them, her trust making me fall even more in love with her. Before I know it, I have a sleeping beauty next to me.

Now the smell of her fear is replaced with the heady scent of *her* - her hair, her skin... all of her. But I swallow hard to clear the odd scent on her skin that's always there after Illion's treatments. Whatever compound he's created to mask her blood type, it works. But now she smells less human, which is not much better, honestly.

The light fades as we cruise down the highway. All that's left of the sun is fiery crimson and orange streaks cutting bright strokes against the cerulean sky. *I wish I could paint it for her.* I wish we could disappear into the deepest part of the Big Thicket and live like the fae with no contact from the outside world. I can almost see our life together. No running or hiding, just living in peace where she could laugh and not panic every time she got so much as a paper cut. That would be fine. Perfect, in fact.

Except, I can't.

The peace between fae and vampire is tenuous at best, and the bargain struck fifty years ago is all that stands between an all-out variant war. If Father suspected I was the one who had stolen his prized possession and taken her into fae territory, that peace would shatter.

I would also risk exposing my mother.

Years of working behind Father's back to undermine his power would be wasted if I am not exquisitely careful. She put herself in so much danger getting Octavia out of the compound. To be fair, so did I, but my mother orchestrated the whole thing so I could play the "I did as I was told" card and live.

She couldn't.

"No," I whisper to myself as if saying it out loud will help, "she couldn't."

"Take her, Seth. Take her and hide her from Cain and your father. You know what will happen to her if you don't. Go! She is the key to my plan and I cannot lose this. We've all worked too hard. Besides, I saw how you look at her. You don't realize it, but I think you care what happens to this girl. She'll be safe with you."

"Mother, I can't just leave you. He'll know exactly what happened if we're both gone."

"Let me handle that. You go. Now!"

And here I am, bringing her back. My head aches behind my eyes, and I feel physically ill. There was a time when I would do anything for my mother, but now that Octavia has my heart, everything I do is for her. All Mother's planning and scheming is about to unravel completely if we are caught, and she'll feel the Grand Master's boot on her neck. My twin brother won't do anything to stop it, either. Hell, he'll probably hold her down.

Octavia snuggles into my arm and sighs in her sleep as Houston's lights flicker in the distance. Her warmth has returned, and I take a moment to soak up the feel of her beside me.

"What am I doing?" I murmur as I place a kiss on the top of her head. Her hair is tangled from her earlier sweat, her scent is still inhuman. I wasn't supposed to fall in love with her, but how could I not?

My phone buzzes on the dashboard, and I jump. Octavia grumbles and twists to the other side of the seat, freeing my arm so I can retrieve the phone before it wakes her up. A black screen with a devil emoji announces the last person I want to speak to.

"Fuck!" I snarl at the phone in my hand, willing myself to answer it. This is the worst timing. I tap the screen and lift it to my ear.

"Cain. What do you want?"

7

LAND OF CONFUSION

Octavia

"Cain."

The hottest boy I have ever seen flashes a brilliant smile. Sunlight filters through the trees as I look up from the forest floor. The light dances through his brown curls, and I wait for the orchestral music to begin because this has to be a movie or a dream. He kneels in front of me, soulful brown eyes radiating concern.

I'd tripped on a fallen branch a second earlier and was checking for scratches when he appeared on the trail. I could've sworn I was alone. *I wasn't bleeding,* thank God, but now my heart was racing like a jackrabbit for an entirely different reason.

"Are you hurt?"

"*No.*" *My ankle throbs, but I ignore it and stand just as he tries to reach out, presumably to help check my leg. He smiles and rises instead, holding out his hand.*

"*As I said, I'm Cain. You are?*"

He's not incredibly tall, but I'm only five foot two, so everyone looks tall to me. I don't recognize him, but I also don't know many people. Sixteen years of house arrest make socialization difficult. My synapses fire, and I remember my training.

"*Abigail.*" *I smile, ignoring his hand and brushing the leaves off my joggers. My ponytail has gone askew, so I pull the scrunchie out of my dark blonde hair and re-tie it. "Nice to meet you.*"

I turn back toward the trail but look in a direction opposite my home - the one I just snuck out of for a clandestine run. "Thanks for checking on me. I have to go."

Turning, I start down the trail. I want to look behind me to see if he's still there, but I resist the urge. One step. Two breaths. I listen for footsteps behind me, but all I hear are the birds and the quiet hum of cars in the distance. Finally, I can't help but glance over my shoulder. He's gone.

"*Nice try, Octavia.*"

I yelp in surprise as he grabs my arms and pulls me to his chest. He leans down as I struggle against his grasp, his lips by my ear.

"*Oh, my. You are* divine,*" he breathes.*

"*Cain!*"

The woman's voice comes from behind - her feet crunching on the leaves. She yanks me from his grasp. I can see his face now, which isn't so cute anymore. Fangs protrude from his upper gums, and those soft brown eyes are drowning in dark pools of shadow. Adrenaline surges, revving my heart, roaring in my ears, and I am shaking uncontrollably.

"Get yourself together, girl," the woman growls. "This goes better for you if you aren't amped up."

Cain takes a step back, and his features soften as he gains distance away from me. His fangs recede, but the shadows around his eyes linger despite the darkness surrounding us. He rips his stare from me and focuses on the woman behind me. "Her parents?"

My breath leaves me in a rush, the roar in my ears turning to a high-pitched ringing that is building in my ears - the thin, keening noise growing louder and threatening to shut me down.

"On their way in. Mae and Albert grabbed them five minutes ago." The woman jerks me around and begins pushing me back down the trail. I can't engage my legs; I am nearly catatonic with terror as I stumble forward. Cain catches up to us, brushing past as he gets ahead of me.

"It's impressive you've lasted this long, Octavia. The last lurker we found was only seven." He tosses a glance over his shoulder, his smile bordering on maniacal, the shadows still clinging to his lashes. My heart is hammering so hard I'm sure I'm having a heart attack. I want to scream or cry, but

to what end? They have my parents, and now they have me. No one will come to help me - no one cares.

After sixteen and a half years of hiding, it's over.

I feel a jab in my arm, my yelp trapped behind clenched teeth. The trees lengthen, and the entire forest twists like putty. My legs go numb, and breathing feels unnecessary. Every muscle in my body struggles to move like they are made of lead..

"Be proud, sweetness! You will go from basic bitch to legendary." He laughs. "A true Cinderella story!"

Then everything goes black.

My eyes snap open, and lock on Seth. I search his face, his body, and for a moment, my mind cannot find the place where Cain ends and Seth begins.

Cain, Seth's twin brother, is the Directorate's consolation prize. Famous for questionable activity, even for a vampire, he's supposedly the opposite of Seth.

Something spooked Seth yesterday at Illion's. He took off, he said, to lead something or someone away from me. Now, we are heading straight for Houston with a "mom will help us" story, and he's answering his brother's phone call like there's some sort of plan.

My eyes dart from Seth, to the road, then to the door beside me. My faith in everything I have believed is shaken by tremors of doubt. Nausea rolls over me as I look harder at him and realize I can't be sure of *anything*. I have only spent a few minutes with his brother, but they are identical twins, and if memory serves me correctly, *identical* is an understatement. Only one defining trait separates them, and I can't test my theory without ensuring my demise.

"See you in a bit."

He glances at me, then tosses his phone on the dashboard. I push myself against the door as hard as possible while my hand finds the door handle.

I'll jump before he takes me.

"Tavi," he starts, before realizing I have the door handle half-pulled. "Hey! What are you doing?"

"You answered Cain's call. He knows we're coming." My voice is shaking. My body is trembling.

"Yeah, I-" his eyes widen, "Oh no, Tavi. No. I said 'I'll be there.' He was pressuring me about the next meeting." He lets off the gas and points the car onto the gravel shoulder of the road.

Every muscle in my body locks. "Keep driving." I'm really trying to sound brave, but I can feel the cold wash of panic rising.

"You are freaking me out, Tavi." He sits straighter in his seat, the speedometer steadily climbing, and reaches for my hand. "It has to be Illion's treatment. It's got you spooked."

How could I not *see it?* My heart is in my stomach like I just took a swan dive off Mount Everest. It's so obvious now. Seth has been playing me while Illion has been doing God knows what to me and calling them "treatments".

Maybe he's collecting my blood while I'm knocked out. Maybe that's why the effects of the treatment are still lingering–I'm weak from blood loss.

That asshole vampire must have always had an agenda, so it wouldn't be a stretch to think he'd been siphoning me for the Directorate. Why would I be so naive as to think the big, bad, vampire scientist was helping me, a coveted delicacy, avoid recapture?

I'm so stupid.

I squeeze my eyes shut. We're going at least seventy miles an hour, so it would be quick if I jumped. I reason with myself to quell the terror, but it's not working. It's funny how death is frightening, even after years of living on its doorstep. I will not go back.

"They won't get me," I whisper, pulling the handle.

8

ONE WRONG MOVE

Octavia

"Tavi!"

I'm falling backward and, surprisingly, I'm not afraid. There's no going back. No escaping the inevitable. The wind screams in my ears, and I can feel my hair whip along the asphalt.

Then I'm back in the car.

He's got me by the arm, the terror on his face convincing. The door is still open, but the wind has almost closed it, the roar deafening in the quiet car. I fall toward him as he yanks the steering wheel and pulls off the highway.

"What are you doing?!" he shouts, his eyes wild and panicked. The car jerks to a sudden stop. "Why would you do that?"

My eyes flick toward the phone in the center console. He lets go of my arm, and I scramble backwards against the partially latched door, one hand reaching behind my back to find the handle again. Seth scrubs his face with his hands, dropping his head before wrapping them back around the steering wheel. Then he looks up at me with those big brown eyes full of worry and fear. "Oh my God, you think I'm working with Cain. Babe, that treatment is messing with your head."

"Then what was that?" I point to the phone.

"What do you think I do when I go home, Tavi?" Agitation colors his voice. He lifts his head to stare at the road, setting his jaw in a hard line.

I honestly don't know the answer. Our policy has always been "the less Octavia knows, the better".

"Go to Council meetings..." I offer, my voice hushed.

"Yeah!" he nods. "I pretend I'm *normal*." He's gripping the steering wheel so hard I think it might break. Seth's voice comes out in a harsh whisper. "And I feed on what I can."

I lower my eyes, shame settling over me like a heavy coat. He's on my side—always has been, and I'm losing my mind if I think otherwise. He can't feed on me because I'm not normal either. A-neg blood, the only thing ninety-nine point nine percent of vampires can drink, is lethal to him. He's an anomaly - that's the only way we can be together. The only reason he has unregulated access to other blood types is because of his family name. Any other vampire would have to hunt illegally or face starvation, but as far as he knows, he's the only one still living.

Technically, he shouldn't even be alive. If a vampire was found to be able to prey on the rest of the population, it would destroy what peace exists. The Directorate diligently works to keep humans subdued by ensuring that their contribution to vampire survival is only six and a half percent of the population—a small price to pay for Directorate protection from all the other mundane evils in the world.

In return, they do their part to keep criminals off the streets and contribute to society like any other big benefactor would. Society is Gotham, and they're a questionable Bruce Wayne family business, of sorts. Anomalies like Seth aren't allowed to exist because his less discerning palate threatens that accord.

"That visit at Illion's was too close for comfort, so we are going to see my mother. We can't keep doing this. *You* can't keep doing this."

He's right, but his mother? He's lost his mind. It's official.

He slides his palm beneath my hand, and the familiar warmth soothes my fractured thoughts. The last three years have been a nightmare to navigate. I live every moment knowing what waits for me if I am caught. Even when I sleep, I am plagued by the memory of my brief captivity. The insane part is that I am being protected by a member of the very family that wants my body for their own sick pleasure. Keep your friends close, but your enemies closer? Yeah, that's me.

Even though we've been together all this time, I know practically nothing about his family; Seth has purposefully kept details from me. Now I want to know everything. But right now I need a minute to recover. I have to get my head straight before I agree to waltz into the belly of the beast that wants to eat me up, literally.

Movement catches my eye as Seth eases back in his seat and pulls me towards him, grabbing my other hand.

"Octavia." His tone is insistent, his face imploring. "You have to trust me. I would do anything to protect you." His brown eyes are still laced with worry.

Holy hell. Those eyes get me every time. Exactly like Cain's, but there's something different that keeps the fear at bay. Maybe it's the delicate flecks of gold scattered in his irises, or maybe it's that those eyes have never looked at me like an object to covet.

"I trust you. I-"

His kiss cuts me off. His fingers curl in my hair, grounding me in *this* reality, not the terror-filled scenes playing out in my head. Seth's lips are tender, his touch treating me as though I might break. I'm drowning in him, the world falling away. I taste the tang of his tongue caressing mine - my heart beats wildly as I surge towards him. We could stay by the side of the road all night, and I wouldn't care. Moments like these remind me why we take this risk of being together. He is my entire world; without him, I am lost.

He pulls away and leans his forehead against mine.

"Sorry," he breathes, his eyes closed and his thumbs stroking my temples. "I'm sorry I scared you."

I kiss him again, then sit back. "Are you *sure* this is safe? I know she's your mother, but she *is* a Dormande."

His jaw feathers. "They didn't give her a choice. My uncle wanted closer to the family's power, and she was his ticket in." He chuckles but shakes his head at the same time. "She'd opposed the Directorate for years before she was married off."

"I bet that made for an interesting childhood," I murmur as I consider this new information. I would never have guessed that his mother was against the very family she married into. But knowing who Seth is, it makes more sense than it should.

"You have no idea. Before my brother and I were born, she openly fought for the humane treatment of donors."

"Donors?" I raise my eyebrows. "You mean victims, right?"

"Sorry," he frowns. "Yes, victims."

The conversation stalls, the air thick between us, and he pulls back onto the road, leaving me to my thoughts. Whenever Seth returns from Directorate gatherings, he slips back into Directorate talk, and he'd just gotten back from a long weekend in Houston when I pulled my latest stunt. He has to put on a show when he's there, and I should be more understanding, but it's hard to see and hear him act like one of *them*.

I look at him through my lashes. He used to have a much harder time shaking it off. I even tried avoiding him for a full day or two because of it. His Directorate mask triggered trauma I didn't want to deal with.

I think about saying something, but I couldn't get the words out if I tried. What would I say anyway? He is quiet - probably wondering how he will get me into the city undetected. I stay trapped in myself, the effects of Illion's treatment lingering, scared shitless to drive into the city. I scrunch down in the seat, keeping my head low as I watch every car we pass, wondering if they already know we are here. We might as well put a siren on Seth's car and advertise.

He drops my hand and opens the glove compartment in front of me. A pair of long gloves tumbles onto the floorboard by my feet. "Put those on, would you?"

"Okay."

No argument here. I'm getting nervous, and he knows it, which means I'll start chewing on my fingernails any moment now - yet *another* opportunity for my blood to spill. I wrinkle my nose at them, but I slip my hands into the thin, supple leather and hold them out in front of me. Seth watches from the corner of his eye, and I catch the lines in his forehead softening. His jaw loosens as he relaxes his death grip on the steering wheel. He jerks his head over his shoulder.

"My hoodie is on the back seat. You should grab it." Awkwardly shuffling around, I snatch the dark grey fabric from the back, but as I turn back to the front, my stomach lurches and my head spins. I clamp my mouth closed and inhale sharply through my nose. The feeling is so intense I slam my palm on the dashboard to steady myself. I cannot throw up. Not in his car. If so much as a single capillary burst from the strain, it would be just as bad as openly bleeding.

"Whoa, you okay?" Seth reaches for my shoulder, dividing his time between watching the road and ensuring I'm not cratering. I collapse against the passenger door and press my head against the cool glass.

"I - I'm just tired." I try to sound as normal as possible. I don't want to alarm Seth, but I don't feel right. Treatments have always drained me, but this time it's different - like my insides are at war with each other. "I'm just a little lightheaded, and my stomach is queasy, that's all. Did we grab my medicine?"

"Yes, and I have Zofran in the center console, too," he says in the same quiet voice he uses when I wake at Illion's. Every day, I take a daily dose of medication provided by Illion. Maintenance medicine, he calls it. We have medications stashed all over the place - we're like the anti-vampire detection A-team.

"I'm good," I reassure him as I lean forward and pull the hoodie over my head, covering me head-to-toe and protecting me from any surprise injuries. The soft fleece warms me up, and it smells like Seth, so, I pull my knees up to my chest and return to resting my head against the window. The landscape whizzes past, dense forest thinning out into patches of trees interrupted by gas stations and the odd house or two set back off the road. It'd be calming if I weren't so scared.

This plan will backfire, I am sure of it, but I don't want him to know how I feel. He is such an optimist. Whereas I have always played the part of the realist, even if Seth insists it is pessimism. But seriously, what could his mother do to help? If I am being honest with myself, I am not convinced he's been able to keep me a secret. Surely she knows about me, and we are driving toward a complete disaster. My limbs feel like rubber, and there's a hollow space in my brain where there used to be hope. The truth is that I could be "collected" before tomorrow; honestly, I'm too drained to protest.

In the distance, I can see the tall buildings of downtown Houston. Though they represent danger, the glittering skyline is still pretty against the twilight sky. They are still far on the horizon, so I know we have another hour or two left in the car. I close my eyes and try to get a little rest. Seth's phone buzzes again, but he silences it and tosses it onto the dashboard before shifting the car into a higher gear.

"Okay, so we are going to see you mother." We are heading into dangerous territory, so I need to know everything I can. "Does she know about me? Does she know what Cain was doing to me?" Dumb question. How could she not know her other son is a monster?

"She knows." My head swims. The motion of the car reminds my body of how awful I feel. I try to mask my discomfort, but I fail miserably. He reaches out for me; this time, I take his hand. He squeezes three times.

I. Love. You.

I can't remember when we started our little love language code, but it offers reassurance. He's not trying to prove anything. He just is the Seth I know. Not Cain—just the Seth that I have to accept has a few extra secrets.

We both stay quiet until the Houston city limits sign whizzes by. The skyscrapers rise like columns of bright, glittering crystal.

With my hand still in his, Seth points to the tallest building. "That's where we're going."

The top three floors glow with a soft, warm ambiance, while lights from a helicopter pad pulse at the top of the building.

"Perfectly safe," I mumble.

It's not long before we wind through the streets of downtown. He turns sharply down a dark alley where one side of a waiting double garage door gapes wide open.

The headlights flick off just as the door closes behind us. Nervous as I am, I keep my mouth shut while he climbs out and pulls the string to turn on a dim, flickering lightbulb. Beside us, I see an older model pickup truck, surprised something so mundane would be owned by the Directorate. He opens the passenger door and gestures to me to follow him.

"The garage at the tower will scan my Mustang and alert everyone that I'm here. We'll take this one to keep from being noticed right away."

In the space of two minutes, we are pulling out of the garage in a truck that smells like fuel and auto parts; It's definitely not a vehicle you would expect from the Directorate.

"I still can't understand why you think your mother will help me," I say as I stare out the window. The buildings crowd together, blocking the top floors from my view. It's only seven o'clock, but the streets are quiet, only putting me more on edge. "Why would she, really?"

"Why wouldn't she?" He turns abruptly into a garage entrance at the base of his family's building, following the narrow drive down one level and pulling into a dark, isolated parking space. "She helped me save you."

9
MOTHER, MOTHER

Genevive Dormande

"Mrs. Dormande?"

Looking out the window thirty-three floors above the downtown Houston streets, my late afternoon view is mottled by clouds threatening the evening with rain. But, in seconds, the sun breaks through in several patches, making a convincing case for a mild night. I shift my focus from the view to my fingers resting against the glass. A ruby the size of an almond sparkles in an errant beam of sunlight. I sigh, dropping my hand to my side.

"Mrs. Dormande?"

"Yes, Evie?" I don't turn around. My assistant, unfazed by my inattention, crosses the room to stand just behind me. Her ability to maneuver effortlessly around my moods is the sole reason she is still here.

"Mr. Dormande will be in attendance this evening. Is there anything special you'd like to wear for dinner?"

I snort most indelicately as I close my eyes and tilt my head back. *Arthur doesn't give a damn about what I wear*. He hardly speaks to me, much less pays attention to my wardrobe.

But I must keep up appearances.

As long as I glitter like an expensive piece of jewelry, he is satisfied.

"Is he bringing guests?"

Evie shuffles through her papers. "I believe so. Let me confirm."

Opening my eyes, I stare at the ceiling. That was a stupid question; of course, he's bringing guests. Why else would he travel into the city? The only question is whether he wants to intimidate someone or put on the appearance of being the quintessential family man.

"Yes," Evie says under her breath as she wrestles a paper out from the stack in her hands. "Dr. Anoterie and the director of the Houston collection facility will be in attendance. Dinner is to be served at seven."

It's to be intimidation then.

If Arthur had opted to host at the collection facility, it would have been to interrogate them about the numbers. They must be falling, or he wouldn't notice. And of course he brings them to my home to do his dirty work. *He does this to get under my skin.* I shake my head and laugh under my breath as I turn away from the window.

"Choose something dark. I'm in a mood."

My spine stiffens. Evie is at the door. She still tries to listen through the heavy wood. *Silly girl.* I can hear hand when she rests it on the doorknob. She hesitates before she raps lightly on the door. "Mrs. Dormande?"

"Come in." I almost answer too quickly.

Evie opens the door, finding me still seated at my dressing table, not quite ready to begin my evening of impersonation. She seems pleased I have followed her recommendation and put on the red and black wraparound dress. I've pulled my rich brown hair up in an elegant twist, stray curls falling delicately around my face. I would rather have it down so I can hide my stray expressions of disgust, but this dress demands an exposed neckline. I lift my chin and examine my reflection from all angles. It would be a crime to hide it. Anything I can do to make Arthur regret making me hate him is a must.

"I've brought these as well," Evie offers. She withdraws the velvet box and sets it near the other jewelry chests on the dresser, popping it open and stepping back. She knows how much I loathe Arthur's shows of matrimonial allegiance, so Evie purposefully chose the ruby and onyx earrings worn by my long-dead best friend, Anabella - Arthur's first love.

I smirk and cast her a devious look. "This is why I adore you, my dear."

She smiles but quickly composes her expression.

"What is it?" I pause before reaching for the jewelry, but still Evie hesitates. "Tell me."

"I received a message from security a few moments ago. Your son was seen entering the garage."

I fasten the earrings and stand. "Seth or Cain?"

As if I had to ask. Cain never visits me.

"Seth."

"Were we expecting him?"

"If we were, I was not aware." Evie shrugs.

"Well," I take a moment, fixing a stray curl, then brush past my assistant. "Arthur cannot know he is here." I look over my shoulder. "But you already know that."

Evie nods.

"Bring him through my private elevator and have him wait here."

"Yes, ma'am." Evie starts for the door, but before she can open it, I stop her.

"Have Clara make him a plate and bring him a small decanter of O, if you would, please. He is so damn stubborn about staying fed, and that should help to keep Arthur from picking up the scent."

"There's another thing, ma'am..." Evie hesitates. "He's brought a girl."

I close my eyes. Things must be out of hand if he'd risk bringing Octavia here. It was only a matter of time, though. Three years was longer than I thought it would last. I purse my lips, inhale a long breath through my nose, and smooth down my dress. If Arthur wants to spring this dinner on me, I'll surprise him with something of my own.

"I've changed my mind." I turn and stride across the room to the door of my expansive closet. "Make the girl comfortable in here and be sure she understands to stay put until one of us comes for her."

"Yes, ma'am."

I scan the dressing room then grab a small, jeweled perfume bottle, spraying two quick pumps in the air. "Make Seth as presentable as you can and bring him to the dining room." Before I leave, I level my gaze at Evie. "Have you fed today?"

Evie nods. "Yes - about an hour ago. All the household staff have, I believe."

"Good." I make for the bedroom door and beckon for Evie to follow. "I wouldn't want you in a position of being unnecessarily tempted."

"I'll be fine," Evie assures me.

"Very well then." We both step into the hallway, and I square my shoulders, striding down the corridor, Evie following closely behind. "Arthur won't know what to do with himself - having to actually behave like a father." I scoff. "As if he even knows what that looks like."

"And Seth, ma'am? I'm certain he will not be thrilled to be in his father's presence."

"Oh, I know he won't, but he has a part to play, and he is acutely aware of my expectations." I wave Evie off as she nears the front sitting room. "Go fetch my son and the girl. We'll be waiting."

I watch as she disappears down the corridor. When she is out of sight, I cross my arms over my chest as I lean heavily against the wall. *What have you done, Seth? I wasn't ready for her yet. Why didn't you warn me?* I take a deep breath, smoothing my dress along my thighs. Whatever the reason, it is time to put on the performance of a lifetime—too much is on the line.

10

RUNNING WITH THE WOLVES

Seth

To be perfectly honest, I have no idea if my mother can help us. But she's the best option we have, and I refuse to let Octavia know my reservations about showing up unannounced. I watch the way she's sitting, how, despite the gloves, she's picking at her fingers without realizing it. She's brimming with anxiety by the time I pull into the parking garage beneath my family's tower.

A knock on my window startles Octavia. She shrinks into the oversized sweatshirt - a signal that she'll keep quiet.

"Mr. Dormande?" The voice is muffled through the window, giving me a chance to slip back into the mask I hate. A man's face peers in, but the shadows make it difficult to tell who it is; though as I roll the window down, there's no mistaking who it is.

"Good evening, Beck." My shoulders relax, and I prop my elbow on the open window's edge. I'm relieved, and I can only hope Octavia picks up on it.

"Evening, sir. You'll need to come with me." Beck backs away from the car as I open the door and step out. Beck leans over to peer inside, then straightens. "Your friend as well. Mrs. Dormande's orders."

"That was fast. How'd she know I was here?"

"Dev saw your car on his way into town."

I glance over my shoulder, giving Octavia a reassuring nod. She blinks in response, and instead of opening her door, she crawls across the bench seat and unfolds herself out of the driver's side door. Her face is a mask of apprehension and tentative trust in me. But as Beck walks toward a dark corridor, Octavia's face softens with relief. I motion for her to follow and reach for her hand, which she grabs and holds onto for dear life.

I'm worried the darkness of the corridor feels suffocating to her, but thankfully, the walk is short. We arrive at a small elevator where Beck nods to me, his eyes straying to Octavia before he turns, and leaves us waiting in front of the closed doors. Alone.

"I might need this hand eventually," I whisper and raise our hands. I brush her knuckles with my lips, trying to loosen the death grip she has on me, making my fingers turn a dark shade of red. She offers an apologetic smile while she loosens her grip enough to restore my circulation. I am positive that in no world does she intend to let me go. In any other situation, I might downplay our connection, but not tonight, not ever again.

"What's happening?" she asks as mechanical groans from behind the doors indicate it is on its way down. Her voice trembles, and my heart plummets. I can't help it. She is living on the edge of desperate fear right now. Her knees buckle as she clutches her stomach and gags, trying to hold back a wave of nausea.

In the space of a millisecond, I sweep my arm around her waist, Tavi collapsing into me. There's a whirring hum from the corner where a surveillance camera trains its focus on us, and I fight the rising urge to rip it from the wall.

"Everything is spinning," she mumbles into my chest.

"I've got you," I murmur into her hair as I second-guess my decision to come here. The only thing keeping me from scooping her up and jumping back in the truck is my unflagging faith in my mother. I try to use the tone of my voice to soothe her, and soon, her racing heartbeat begins to slow.

"You've got me," she repeats, then whispers against my chest, "You are so strong."

She's fading, and gut-wrenching fear surges in my chest. This looks like so much more than post-treatment Octavia making me seriously question what Illion has done this time, but he said that every dose is a risk, and the stress of being here isn't helping things. Keeping one arm around her waist, I splay my hand wide across her stomach, trying to give her a sense of security.

I place a desperate kiss against her clammy temple. "I know you don't believe me, but you are safe. I promise."

I feel her flinch when the elevator door slides open, the bright light surrounding us a stark contrast to the shadowy corridor. A petite young woman in a stylish charcoal-grey pantsuit waits for us inside.

"Evie." My reflexive recoil is impossible to hide, and Octavia grips my shirt when she feels me take a step back, one shoulder curling forward in front of her protectively. "Where is my mother?"

I angle myself even further, putting more distance between us and the woman in the elevator.

"She sent me to collect you." Her voice is crisp with the slightest hint of an accent. "We have unexpected company this evening, Mr. Dormande. Your mother has given me specific instructions. Now," she steps to the side, "please come with me. We need to be quick about it."

"Seth?" Octavia looks up at me, trying to gauge my expression, but I have my mouth set in a hard line to hide my trepidation. She's sweaty and pale. I can play tough all I want, but I am afraid she will completely black out any second. *What am I doing?* Evie says nothing, but she does not take her eyes off Octavia. I inch back until we are pressed up against the opposite side of the elevator and keep my eyes fixed on Evie. Even half-breeds have vampiric reflexes. She's fast, but I'm faster.

"I've already fed, Mr. Dormande," she says matter-of-factly. "She is perfectly safe."

Some of Octavia's rigid tension releases, but she has not completely relaxed. She won't until we're driving away.

"What do I call her? Octavia? Tavi?"

Before I can answer, Octavia raises her head.

"You don't"

I recognize the snark I love so much in her voice, and my shoulders relax. I feel her ease back so she can stand on her own, and a quick glance down at her face reveals her stubborn streak coming to life.

Evie eyes us as the elevator clears one floor after another, the whoosh of each level accentuating the awkward silence.

Finally, we come to a stop, and the door slides open, revealing an opulent bedroom. Octavia tries to stand straighter and lift her chin, but it isn't long before she's leaning against me again.

Evie hastily ushers us to my mother's closet, the room almost the same size as our entire house. Racks of clothes, shoes, and every handbag available line the walls. In the center of the space is a deep green velvet chaise lounge. My mother, as anti-Directorate as she is, does love her wardrobe.

"Mr. Dormande, you are to come with me. Your mother requires your presence in the dining hall. The guests will arrive soon, and you are expected for dinner."

I don't buy that, not one bit. Octavia sags in my arms, her eyes fluttering closed, her breathing shallow.

"*Expected?* Nobody knew I was coming. Try again."

Evie sighs in exasperation. "As your arrival was unannounced, your mother now expects you to attend dinner. Your father is bringing guests, and Mrs. Dormande would appreciate your assistance in hosting during their stay."

I stop, Octavia trembling in my arms. Twisting around, I shoot a glare at Evie. "My *father*?"

"Yes. He's hosting some of the collection facility leadership."

Oh, hell no.

I tighten my hold on Octavia and prepare to return to the elevator. I am not participating in this.

Has my mother lost her mind?

"I'm not leaving Tavi here alone." I don't take my eyes off Octavia as I lower her to the cushions. Once she is settled, I kneel beside her and tuck a strand of her hair behind her ear. She is terrified, so I unclasp my wolf-head bracelet and slip it on her wrist. "See, I'll be right here with you." My thumb lingers on her wrist, concern thrumming through me as the iciness of her skin. She opens her eyes, flicking a worried, glazed glance in Evie's direction.

I follow her gaze, watching Evie working her jaw, frustration evident in her taut expression. "She'll be fine. She is under your mother's protection and, in this house, your mother's word is law."

I let my hand slide down to Octavia's shoulder, giving it a squeeze before standing to face Evie. "This is different. This isn't just about my brother now."

"Your mother suspected you were bringing her when I told her you weren't alone. Having Octavia kept in here was by her design." Evie beckons me to follow her. "She will be safe with me."

Evie has been in my mother's service for several years and has earned her trust. She has never given me a reason to doubt her, though in light of this new situation, my trust in anyone is monumentally hard to find.

"What about Dev and Beck?" I know the answer, but it makes me feel better to ask.

"We all are loyal to your mother. If she has kept your secret, then we have too." Evie steps back to let me pass. "Keeping her safe in here will not be the biggest challenge tonight," she adds under her breath.

"Seth." Octavia's voice sounds so small. Tears spill from her eyes as she feebly reaches for me. "Please don't leave me here alone. You can't leave me here."

My heart rips into pieces. *This was stupid*, I tell myself, preparing to gather her up and make a break for it. Maybe hiding amongst the fae wasn't such a bad idea after all.

"He doesn't have a choice."

The voice stops me in my tracks as my mother walks through the door and takes me by the arm. She fixes her eyes on Octavia, lifting her chin and staring down her nose.

"You are intriguing, young lady, but you are the least of my concerns right now."

11
POLICY OF TRUTH

Seth

THE DINING ROOM IS dim, the candles on the table casting faint, flickering shadows on the walls. Mother sits at the end of the table, just next to the head seat - that spot is reserved for my father. I am cleaned up and dressed in a stylish, modern jacket and collarless shirt provided by my mother, but I can't help squirming in my seat next to her.

"You do this all the time," Genevive hisses under her breath. "What problem is there with one more night?"

"I am able to do this, to play the role of dutiful son, because Tavi's as far away from this hellscape as possible, not stashed in a closet down the hall." I clear my throat and sit back, finding it difficult to behave normally. I glance at my mother. "What am I supposed to say when he asks why I'm here? I just told everyone I was leaving the country two days ago. Shouldn't we have talked about this first?"

"Just say you missed your flight." Genevive nervously chuckles as she toys with the bracelet on her wrist. "He never asks anyway."

"I'm never unexpectedly here."

"He's so self-absorbed, he won't notice."

Even though I never wanted anything to do with my father, her comment still stings. Mother sheltered me throughout my entire childhood, shielding the family from my inability to consume the blood everyone else required. My father always thought I was simply sickly and weak, never bothering to spend enough time with me to learn the truth. Cain was the attention whore anyway, so it worked in my favor. My only interaction with my father is my monthly appearance at the Directorate council meeting, and it is dismissive at best. My asshole brother is his golden child; the heir raised in his image.

Voices from outside the dining room catch our attention, the two of us stiffening in our seats. I bristle at the sound of my father's subdued, sinister voice.

"Why am I really here, Mother?" As much as I hate it, my heart pounds loud enough I'm sure Father can hear. "You said I would be free of him as long as I played my part."

Genevive raises her hand to silence me as more voices become audible. There are several I don't recognize. Then another, more familiar, joins in and chills crawl down my spine, the hair on my neck standing tall. My fear is validated when the group of men and women enters the room, and Illion saunters in with them. I know he works for my father, but according to him, his involvement was always at a distance. This can't be good.

Our eyes meet.

My heart hammers in my chest. If they couldn't hear it before, they certainly can now.

Illion always maintained his dealings with the Directorate were peripheral, that he did outside research, but here he is looking like he's a part of my father's inner circle. Illion lets his eyes wander around the room, showing no emotion until they land on me. He tilts his head in acknowledgement, a smirk spreading across his thin, gaunt face.

Oh God.

As my nerves fully ignite, my heart rate skyrockets, and I chance a glance at my mother. Her eyes widen only slightly, but there is no mistaking her surprise.

Arthur winds his way around the table, ignoring my mother, and stops just behind me. He places his long, slender hands on my shoulders and squeezes less than gently. He is a tall, lean man — his face nothing but sharp angles and shadows.

"To what do we owe this extra visit, *son*?"

The room quiets, and I stiffen.

Here's to winging it.

"I missed my flight. Since I was in town, I decided to stop in and visit Mother. I missed seeing her before I left." It's the best I could come up with. I try to sound casual, but I am failing.

"Ah yes, *your mother.*" Arthur releases me and sidles over to Mother, who lifts her chin and glances up in her husband's direction.

"Should a son not visit his mother once in a while?" Her fake smile is obvious to everyone in the room. She's trying to bait him into an argument to get him off my back. They've played this game since I was a child. "At least he *wants* to see me."

Arthur pauses, then continues past her chair and stands behind his own at the head of the table. "I'm sure he missed your coddling, no doubt."

"Seth? No, Arthur. Seth and I have a relationship." She places one elbow on the table and leans in his direction, resting her chin in her hand. "That thing two people have when they respect one another?" She sits back and tucks her hands in her lap. "I know this is difficult for you to understand." There is no mistaking the venom in her voice.

My father holds his dark gaze on her for a long, silent moment before rearranging his face into a warm and welcoming smile.

"No more family talk. Welcome, guests!" He gestures to the chairs around the table as he sits in the ornately carved armchair. "Please take your seats."

The men and women shuffle around, quickly finding their places around the table. Most of the guests have worry etched in their eyes. All except Illion. His are locked on mine. I can't help but stare as the older vampire saunters toward his seat.

I tear my attention away when the serving staff enters the room and begins pouring thick red liquid into the tumblers at each place setting. One server approaches Illion, and he raises his hand to stop her.

"I prefer mine over ice."

She nods and scurries away with his glass.

The other server, finishing his rounds, pours my mother's glass and gives me an apologetic smile. "I'm out, Mr. Dormande. Allow me to take your glass, and I'll fill it in the kitchen."

"Thank you." I nod and hand over the tumbler. Mother's doing, no doubt. She always keeps a supply I can drink stashed away. Only a select number of staff know how to manage my situation, and they're carefully controlled by her. The server returns with my glass and quickly scuttles away as Arthur stands.

"Thank you, ladies and gentlemen, for joining me here tonight. I've provided you with the best of my private stock, and," he lifts the tumbler, admiring the dark liquid and the fog forming on the glass, "*nous ne voudrions pas gâcher le dîner avec du sang de qualité inférieure*." He raises the glass. "Only the best. To the Directorate and the fine people who keep it in operation."

"To the Directorate," the group echoes with palpable uncertainty, raising their tumblers. Illion halfheartedly lifts his own, the large cubes sloshing in the thickening blood. My mother sits back, her hands neatly folded in her lap, raising an eyebrow when I reach for my glass.

She nods with a subtle drop of her chin. Arthur takes the first sip and smiles, savoring the thick, warm liquid. The others do the same. My mind shifts to Octavia before I release a shaky breath and put the glass to my lips.

My mother has never failed me. I close my eyes and let the warm, syrupy liquid roll over my tongue. She will not fail Octavia.

As it slithers down my throat, I already know. I'm drinking A-negative. My throat immediately begins to constrict, but I do my best to maintain control.

"My dear Genevive," my father purrs. "Aren't you thirsty?"

She places one hand on my arm, sensing my distress. "I've already had my fill, Arthur."

Instinct supersedes caution, and she turns toward me. Try as I might to keep control, my eyes go wide and my face tingles.

"Seth!" she breathes, panic lacing her words.

Arthur places his hands on the table and leans toward us.

"You've kept his secret well, wife, I'll give you that. But how dare you think yourself smarter than me?"

I feel the telltale tremors that come before the seizure. Mother shoves her chair back, clutching my face in her hands.

Not helping, Mom.

She frantically looks toward the kitchen door. "Clara!"

"Clara is occupied elsewhere, *dearest*."

My father's words sound distant, and a dull headache radiates from the base of my skull. When the twitching in my hand starts, I know.

The seizure is imminent.

It's been a long time since I've had one, but it's a feeling one does not quickly forget. A pain, like muscles ripping apart, washes over me, and I only half-realize I've slid out of my chair and fallen to the floor, my body going rigid with a life-threatening reaction to the blood I have consumed. Mother, helpless, can only hold on to me while I writhe in agony. She clutches my shoulders and presses her forehead to mine.

"I didn't do this," she whispers.

"Where is she?" A figure is hovering above us, though that makes no sense. My vision is fading, and I'm not entirely positive who it is — maybe my father? "Where is the girl?"

It *is* him.

Mother ignores the question.

"Illion!" my father's voice booms. Out of the corner of my eye, I think I see the shape of Illion's legs flex, straighten, then disappear.

"Take him and stabilize him. I want to speak with him as soon as he is able."

Someone kneels beside me. The room is disappearing from my vision.

"If I *can* stabilize him, sir. The reaction is significant." Illion's tone suggests the request is futile, that I will not survive this.

Bony hands rest on my neck. My mother is forced away from me, and I feel more hands on my taut, jerking body. "I'll need to take him to our facility first, and then to my lab."

I should be afraid, but I don't care where he is taking me. The only fear I have is for Octavia. She cannot be here without me. I fight to stay conscious.

"Do what you must."

My father leans down and sniffs the air above me. He straightens and gestures to someone.

"Take Mrs. Dormande to her room. I'll be right behind you."

They reach for Mother, ripping her away from me and quickly overpowering her. The two men sneer and make their way through the door as my vision fades. Before they disappear down the hall, Arthur calls out, "And bring a team in to search the penthouse. She's here. I can smell her on him."

12

RUN TO THE HILLS

Octavia

Something's wrong.

The woman named Evie has been pacing in front of the locked door, driving me crazy ever since Seth and his mother disappeared. I'm already a hot mess, not to mention whatever else Illion has done to me -I don't need her escalating my freak out; thank you very much. I peel the gloves off my hands to try and alleviate the suffocating claustrophobia of being held in a closet. It doesn't help.

Evie stops abruptly, pressing a finger against her ear. Her brow furrows, then, even though I thought her eyes couldn't be any bigger than they already are, they widen. Faster than I thought possible, she's beside me and jerking me to my feet, gathering the gloves and shoving them into her pocket. This closet is dimly lit, so it's no wonder that I stumble over one leg of the chaise.

"Wai-"

She cuts me off by putting one finger in front of her lips. There's no mistaking her urgency as we scurry into a rack lined with coats—so many coats. Odd. We're in the coastal bend of Texas, and winter only lasts two weeks here. No one in Houston wears a coat like this.

There's a subtle click, and I'm dragged into a narrow opening in the wall, which closes immediately behind us. My life is in imminent danger, but I can only think of Narnia.

What is wrong with me?

We haven't stopped moving since we squeezed into the narrow passageway. Evie tugs harder on my arm and I yank it back, breaking her hold.

"What's happening? What's wrong?" I keep my voice low, painfully aware something is wrong, but I want answers before I get further away from Seth.

"No time," she whispers as she keeps moving. "Stay with me. That bastard got the jump on us."

I can't see anything except a faint blue glow in front of Evie. Even then, I need to squint to see anything clearly. I'm not getting left behind in a vampire nest *inside a wall*, so I push on after her. Everything in me wants to turn and go back to Seth, but it is so dark, I don't think I could find the doorway back. I don't have a choice right now, so I follow her. We make our way through a turn, and she stops. One hand is back up beside her ear.

"Clara?" She waits, listening intently. Her lips thin, then she tries again. "Clara?" I count three seconds, still weirdly transfixed by being in the Narnia secret passage. She drops her hand from her ear and punches the wall. "Shit!"

This is insane.

I'm inside a wall that is inside the penthouse of the regional controlling family of vampires, and I am being led away by another vampire who clearly has some sort of death wish. My head spins, and I have to drop my head to slow it down. I reach out and brace my hands on the walls.

I must be tripping.

Maybe Illion's treatment included some extended-release acid. Maybe I never woke up and I'm still strapped to that horrible chair in Illion's basement. I'm open to any explanation, as long as it includes my boyfriend.

Evie glances back at me. "Are you afraid of heights?"

Yep, definitely tripping hardcore donkey balls.

"Octavia!" she hisses, and I snap to attention. "If we don't move now, we are both done. Are you afraid of heights?" She repeats it slowly, emphasizing each word.

What sort of question is that?

"Yes, y-yes," I manage to stutter. I'm terrified of heights, but I don't elaborate - I have no time.

She's already started climbing a flimsy metal ladder I didn't even notice. The blue glow is still in front of her, but the further away she gets, the darker it becomes. As the shadows close in, every worst-case scenario plays in my head.

My hands are shaking as wave after wave of weakness and nausea hit me, but I grab the metal and pull myself up. It's awkward maneuvering in the narrow space, but the confinement keeps the panic down as we climb higher. I can hear her talking again.

"Dev, the roof." Pause. "Yes. Get them here *now!*"

The roof? This is a skyscraper. She can't... I grip the rung till my knuckles go white as my stomach flip-flops.

"I know. The whole building is compromised. That's why we need them."

Them? Hang on. Who is them?"

Her voice drops, turning into a growl. "Just do it."

We continue to climb for what feels like hours to my weak muscles. Finally, she stops and steps onto a narrow landing where the ladder ends. Shimmying to the side, she whispers down to me.

"Up here, Octavia. Squeeze in."

I look up, realizing we've reached the top. There's nowhere else to go. I keep thinking about Seth. My heart is a frenzied mess because I'm getting farther and farther away from him. He didn't want to leave me even though he trusted Evie, but to be fair, he also trusted his mother. ..That was a mistake, or I wouldn't be scrambling through the walls right now.

My arms feel rubbery, and my legs are shaking, but at least we aren't climbing anymore. I have a death grip on the ladder - a good thing because another wave of dizziness hits me and threatens to take me down.

"Oh no, you're not done yet," Evie warns as she yanks me off the ladder and pins me against the wall. "God, Mal said you'd be stronger," she mumbles as she gropes through her pocket. "Here's to hoping he's right."

A sharp sting in my thigh sends rocket fuel through my body. White-hot energy rips through my heart, and I'm ready to launch. She reaches above our heads and yanks on a lever to a concealed hatch. The release of pressure sends it flying open.

Evie is up and out before I know it, reaching back for me with a determined look on her face. Her hair whips around in a frenzy - the wind screaming past the opening. Whatever she's injected into me has taken my fear and slapped a muzzle on it.

I climb.

Emerging onto the roof, I'm nearly blown over by the gusts, managing to catch myself and stand tall. Afraid-of-heights me is entirely aware of what is happening, but jet-fuel me is in control now.

"ETA?" Evie is crouched, shouting as she cups her ear.

I scan the sky, hardly believing where I am. Clouds have rolled in so close I feel like I can reach up and touch them. *It's incredible*. The first drops of rain begin, and I tilt my head back, relishing the feel of the cold. My body feels like it's on fire, and the rain sizzles against it when it hits.

"Octavia!" Evie has to yell so I can hear her through the gale and the rush of adrenaline making my ears throb. "Get down!"

She jerks me into a crouch beside her as rhythmic gusts, strong enough to take my breath away, buffet us till we are nearly bowled over. Two figures streak over our heads and slam into the rooftop, sending sparks flying from beneath their feet. I shake uncontrollably, though not from fear. The jet fuel is spent, and my treatment-ravaged body has had all it can take. As much as I'd like to stare at what just arrived, my eyes glaze over.

"Bas, grab her!"

Large arms scoop me up, and I'm pressed against a giant chest. There's a heartbeat - loud and fast. Powerful, like a diesel engine.

"I've got you." It's more of a rumble than a voice.

My stomach drops, but the rushing wind changes to a steady, rocking sensation that soothes me. Rain pelts my face, but I can't feel the sting. The gusts soften, caressing instead of beating my flesh, and I'm soaked, though I don't feel cold anymore.

I don't know what is happening or whose arms I am in, but I'm completely depleted. I give in to the darkness and let unconsciousness claim me.

13
TROUBLE

Octavia

"CALM NOW, CHILD," a heavily accented voice murmurs.

The first thing I smell when I realize I'm still alive is wood smoke. Voices intermingle in hushed tones, chanting in a language I can't understand. As consciousness returns, so do my racing thoughts. I open my eyes to a crowd of painted faces peering over me. Hands adorned with tattoos shake above me, bracelets of bone and wood rattling as they pass.

I want to jump up and scream — to run away — but my body will not obey. Someone lifts my head and puts a cup to my lips before I even know what is happening.

"Drink dis, now."

Bitter, syrupy liquid slithers down my throat, and I choke, spewing a fair amount all over myself. The chanting gets louder. I'm disoriented, and my chest aches like I can't find oxygen, like I'm drowning. I'm struggling because more hands are on me now, gripping my arm and legs tightly. My unresponsive body feels hot - like it did when Evie injected me on the roof - but it's not jet fuel like before. This feels like I'm boiling from the inside out. Agonizing fever rages and intensifies. Just like when I'm at Illion's, I reach my breaking point and allow unconsciousness to be my escape.

Frog croaks and cricket chirps whisper in my ear. The solemn call of a bird in the distance makes me open my eyes, but the gentle lapping of water against wood is soothing and nearly lulls me back to sleep. In the distance, thunder rumbles, rolling through the night air.

Before I can close my eyes, everything comes back — Illion, Seth, the penthouse, *the rescue on the roof*. Gasping, I sit up.

I'm outside. Or am I? I struggle to lift my legs over the edge of where I lay, realizing too late that I'm in a hammock. I tumble to the ground with a grunt, damp soil smelling of fish bait pressing into my face making my stomach turn. I take a minute to be sure I won't keel over, then sit back on my heels. The moon peeks out from behind gathering clouds, illuminating the tall cypress trees in front of me. Shifting silver light sharpens the ripples in the water until they look like blades.

Where in the hell am I?

"You're at my place, *cher.*"

My eyes widen at the response to my thoughts. It's the same low voice from the roof. Startled, I twist around. The tallest man I have ever seen walks out of the shadows wiping a wicked-looking knife on a rag. His face is chiseled with sharp angles set in a scowl. As he nears, I shrink closer to the ground and his expression morphs into concern.

"*C'est bon, cher, c'est bon.*" He places the knife on a tall worktable and kneels in front of me. He's not wearing a shirt and his skin, dark like honey, glistens with sweat. He's peering at me, worry softening his features. "It's okay."

I don't know what to do. Do I run? Do I talk to him? Clearly, I'm safe because I feel much better than I have in a long time. I've also been left to sleep undisturbed until only a few moments ago. So, I opt for talking, mostly because I don't think I could outrun someone as obviously fit as this guy.

"Where am I?"

Now he smiles, and his whole face relaxes. His eyes are dark green, flecked with gold, and he has an odd slant to the tops of his ears, almost fae-like. He stands, offering his hand as he rises. After a quick hesitation, I take it, surprised by his soft skin.

"You're in Louisiana, *cher*. I brought you here the night before last."

"Louisiana? How? All I remember is the roof, then something huge with wings attacked-"

His barking laugh cuts me off.

"Attacked?" He smirks and shakes his head. "Nah, *cher*, we didn't attack you. We *rescued* you." He turns to the worktable, and my breath escapes in a gasp as I stand.

Folded tightly against his back are wings — not big and feathery like you see in all the movies and TV shows. They similar to the wings of a bat, and they twitch in response to his arm movements. It's almost like they are glistening, and I have the urge to reach out and touch them.

"I can feel you looking, y'know."

Averting my eyes, I struggle to think of something to say that isn't idiotic, but nothing comes to mind.

"You hungry?" He breaks the awkward silence.

I haven't thought about it, but I'm ravenous. I don't think I've eaten anything for three days.

"Starving," I mutter, staring again. His wings are fascinating. At first glance they are simple, but when I look harder, I see the thin skin undulating with amber and onyx. The semi-liquidity is beautiful and terrifying at the same time. I've been aware there are other supernatural beings in the world, of course, but one that can fly? This one is new.

Aside from vampires, the only others I know of are the fae, and that's only because I'm inside so much and have a ton of time to read. Secretive and clannish, they keep to themselves and never bother with the rest of the world. Vampires don't hunt them, and humans are of no value to them, so they might as well not exist.

"Tell you what," he turns with two bowls in his hand. "You eat something, and I'll answer your questions."

The aroma coming from the bowls makes my decision for me. I rush forward to snatch my meal, but he pulls it away. "Ah, now, wait a minute," he laughs. "It's hot!"

He guides me from beneath the shelter to a rough-hewn table and benches, waiting until I've settled in my seat to set a bowl in front of me. Lights are strung through the tree limbs, casting a warm and welcoming glow around the camp. He relaxes his wings as he sits on the opposite bench, and now I can get a better look at him. His gold-shot brown hair is thick and just shy of curly. He has the top part pulled back and tied, but the rest of its length falls just past his shoulders.

"Dig in." He gestures with his spoon, and while every cautious instinct I have screams beware, I need no encouragement. My mouth has been watering ever since I woke..

"Now," he says between bites. "Let's do this right. I'm Bastien."

I look up from my bowl, searching his face. He's got an accent I can't place at first, but then I realize it sounds Cajun. Juice dribbles down my chin, but I don't care. Bastien watches me intently, and I know I should respond to him, but my body is craving nourishment like never before, so I keep eating the rich broth, rice, and sausage.

"Take your time, Octavia," Bastien picks at his food while I finish inhaling my own. My cheeks flush as I glance up and catch his eyes on me.

"Tavi," I whisper. "Seth calls me Tavi." I drop my eyes back to the table and stare at the splintering wood, but my eyes catch a glimpse of Seth's bracelet around my wrist. My brain seizes the opportunity to flash memories of the last time I saw him. I feel his palm pressing against my stomach. I smell his scent wrapping around us. I see the worry he's trying to hide as his mother leads him away.

And then I am spiraling through the fear, the adrenaline, and the rush of everything that happened that night. I try to push it away, feeling the inevitable freak out rising to the surface.

I have absolutely no idea what happened in that tower to cause Evie to do what she did. She put herself in as much danger as I did, so it must have been bad. I have so many questions, I don't know where to begin, and I'm afraid I will regret getting answers if I start asking.

"Okay." I tap my spoon on the side of the bowl while I think, then set it down. "Where's Evie?"

"She went back a while ago with Auralie to see what she could find out." He raises his eyebrows and nods. "You know, that was some dumb luck of y'all's that Aura and I were so close when the call came in. We were practically on top of you." He leans forward on his elbows. "There's a reason Evie brought you here."

"And here I thought it was just to escape certain death," I mutter around the food in my mouth.

"You're funny," he chuckles under his breath. "Seriously, though. Trust her. She doesn't want to lose him, I promise. Or you."

"He's right." A familiar voice comes from around the side of the shack, and I turn to see Evie striding over to the table. She sits down next to me, her back to the table, looking worn out and bedraggled. Her clothes and hair are damp. My brow furrows. She should be in pain from the water. Come to think of it, she should have died on the roof when the rain started.

"You're wet," I whisper, a distant rumble of thunder punctuating my observation. "How are you not hurt?"

"I'm a half-breed." Her tone is clipped as she pulls away. "Those rules don't apply to me."

Before I can process what she's just said, she twists to face Bastien and continues.

"Arthur has Genevive under full security back in her penthouse."

My heart races, and I don't mean to cut her off, but I do. "And Seth?"

"He's not there. We can't get Dev on comms, either." At the mention of Dev, Evie falters but she clears her throat and continues. "Best we can guess, by the vehicles headed north, Illion has him."

"Oh, thank God," I breathe. "Then he's okay."

Evie turns to me with one arched eyebrow, cocking her head to one side.

"He's... he's an ally. He's been helping us for the last three years," I explain.

"Illion helping someone?" Evie snorts. "Now that's a fairy tale if I ever heard one."

On the surface, my brain won't let go of Illion, the unsavory savior, the ally in our fight to keep me safe. As much as I hate him, Seth trusted him with his life. With *my* life. But in the back of my mind, there's a flicker of doubt. I never fully saw what Illion did to me. He gave me the creeps every time we had to see him.

"Fairy tale?" I rock back and swing my leg over the bench to stand up, but stop myself. "What do you mean?"

Evie leans her back against the table. "I don't know what Illion you know, but the one *I* know has a nickname in the Directorate." She folds her arms across her chest and levels a hard stare in my direction. "Dr. Frankenstein."

"Don't you worry, *cher*,"

Bastien is beside me. *When did that happen?* I shrink back in surprise.

"Auralie will get a line on him. Tracking is her specialty."

"There's no one at the facility labs right now; we checked." Evie frowns. "If he has Seth, and we think he does, we don't know where he's taking him."

Visions tumble through my head. The garage and the lab beneath. A chair with worn straps and green tile walls. The chill. The pain. The smell.

"I do," I breathe. "I know exactly where he's going."

14

THE PATRON SAINT OF LIARS AND FAKES

Seth

I SMELL IT BEFORE I see it.

Illion's lab.

I lift my head as far as I can and open my eyes. Green tile blurs with steel cabinets. The acrid scent of alcohol sticks in the back of my throat and stings my nose. I struggle to sit up, stopped by the restraints of the procedure chair — the chair I watched Octavia lay on so many times. The room is dim, just like Illion sets it before her procedures. My immediate reaction is panic.

"Ah, he wakes."

Illion saunters into the room, and I stop trying to keep my eyes open, my head flopping back against the chair. I don't want to see his face. I hear him pacing a slow circle around the procedure chair, and I know he is scrutinizing me, judging me. Chills cascade from my scalp to my fingertips.

"Well done, well done. You survived," he begins, "which means we've got something we can work with." He stops in front of the chair.

"Where is Tavi?" I growl and crack my eyes open. I want to see his face when he lies to me.

Illion's eyebrows rise, and he shrugs. "I do not know. I planned on retrieving that information from you."

"Liar." The word escapes my lips, dripping with as much hate as I can muster. I want to pull free of the restraints, but my muscles don't respond, and it's hard to catch my breath.

He chuckles to himself. "Really, Seth. I have no clue where she is. I left before your father's men found her. I had *urgent matters* to attend to." Illion pulls a rolling stool over and sits, leaning his elbows on the chair and steepling his fingers under his chin. "Though, about an hour ago, I heard they never found her. Arthur is positively furious." He smirks as he drops his chin so his fingers rest against his lips. "Where'd she go, Seth?" His voice is soft now, nearly a whisper. "Who helped her escape this time?"

"How would I know? And if I did, why would I tell you?" My voice is an angry whisper. "You betrayed me. You betrayed her!"

Illion doesn't respond. The buzz of the fluorescent lights grows louder as each second passes. Finally, he stands to retrieve something from the steel cart behind him. I realize, that this is what Tavi has experienced so many times before, and it turns my stomach.

"Let me ask you something." he asks, his back still turned.

I stay quiet, refusing to play his games.

"Why *did* you trust me?" He hums as he turns, a vial of blood in his hands. "Why would I, the leading scientist at the Directorate, aid in the concealment of coveted contraband? Because I *care?*" He chuckles. "Initially, helping you and Octavia was for strictly selfish purposes. I told your mother I would help only because, if she had fallen into the hands of your father, he would have stashed her away for himself. Octavia is an invaluable source for my research, so I couldn't have that."

Illion approaches with the vial in hand and settles himself on the rolling stool again, easing it near the procedure chair. I can't take my eyes off what he's holding. I know it's bad, but *how bad* is the real concern. "By agreeing with your mother's request to help, I had not only a rare specimen, but with you, a one-in-a-million vampire anomaly."

I don't know what hurts more — being played for a fool or being used. But both make me feel hollow inside. I would gladly curl up and die right now if Octavia weren't missing with my father on her tail.

"You lied. You lied this entire time," I growl through clenched teeth.

"I did what was necessary. And now, it is necessary for me to study you, this time, with your father's trust." Illion's smile bordered on diabolical.

"I won't cooperate." I glance down at the vial in Illion's hand. "I won't."

A smile blooms across Illion's face as he pats my shoulder. His thin, bony hand reaches down to my stomach to clutch the edge of my shirt. With a pull, Illion reveals a tube inserted into my abdomen. My eyes go wide as I pull against the restraints while he retrieves a syringe from his coat pocket and draws up the blood, inserting the needle into the port.

"Oh, I know." He nods with feigned empathy as he depresses the plunger. "Now you won't have to."

15

DO YOU BELIEVE IN MAGIC?

Octavia

ANOTHER RUMBLE OF THUNDER rolls across the sky when a powerful blast of wind stirs the trees near us. As I look up, a woman drops out of the sky, and once again, my eyes widen in awe.

She's beautiful in a frightening and powerful way. Like Bastien, her skin is dark, but hers is more molasses than Bastien's rich honey complexion. Her wings have scales, but they have an iridescent sheen, almost insect-like. She walks toward us and stands next to Bastien.

"Penthouse recovery ain't gonna happen anytime soon." She leans forward, the muscles in her arms flexing, and places her hands on the table.

Bastien looks up at her, then back at me. "Octavia-" he stops himself, "I mean... Tavi, this is Auralie."

She nods in my direction, then levels her gaze at Evie's disheveled form. "I still have someone on the inside, no thanks to you. I'm waiting for them to get back to me. But damn, the energy coming off that building," she shakes her head, "*Ça sent mauvais* - the place reeks."

"Why do we care about the penthouse?" I look at the faces around me, getting frantic. My hand taps on the table faster and faster. "You said Seth's not there."

"But Genevive is." Evie stands, and and runs a jerky hand through her hair.

Evie whirls toward Auralie. "What about the Mothers? Can they help?"

"Y'all know they stay as far away from the Directorate as they can," Bastien warns.

"Who else can we ask?" Evie throws her hands up in exasperation. "We can't leave her. He'll kill her."

"Aren't we going to get Seth?"

Evie is looking at Auralie and Bastien is watching both women. I ball my fists, my teeth grinding because no one is listening to me.

The sky flashes, illuminating the low clouds on the horizon.

"But what about Seth?!" Anger roils in my gut, threatening to explode, all the while the three of them keep talking like I'm not standing right here. I suck in a breath and slam my fist on the table, my spoon clattering in my bowl.

They stop talking and turn their heads in my direction, looks of surprise stamped across all of their faces.

It's about damn time.

"What. About. Seth?"

All three drop their eyes, and Evie sighs and sits back down beside me, tracing the woodgrain with her finger.

"Octavia, Genevive has years of secrets that could be the undoing of hundreds, maybe thousands, of people." She touches her chest, her fingers shaking. "Me included. She's been protecting Seth his entire life, but this didn't start with him."

No one will look me in the eye. "What didn't start with him? What are you talking about?" I already mostly understand what they are telling me, but I'm not letting this go. I can't. *He needs me.*

"Cher," Bastien leans across the table and puts his hand on my arm. "Genevive Dormande has been smuggling people like you out of the hands of collectors even before she married into the family."

Auralie walks around the table. "While people like Genevive were hiding humans, the Mothers created our kind," she gestures to Bastien, "as a protection against vampires."

"But that was a long time ago." Bastien's hand slides down my arm, his fingers lacing with my own.

My frantic urgency quells just enough for me to focus, even though all this information feels like too much. All I want to do is find a way to get to Seth. I don't care about anything or anyone else. I'm angry, panicked, worried, and none of what they tell me matters if Seth is in danger.

"If you were made to fight vampires, then let's go get Seth! Illion is old, and probably by himself at the lab. He's just one vampire. It should be easy for you to get him out of there!"

I yank my hand from Bastien and burst to my feet. My eyes cast about for an exit because all I want to do is leave. I want to jump in the first car I can find and drive back to Illion's with one of these magical beings in tow. If they are some kind of all-powerful flying beings, fantastic. *Let's fucking roll.*

"Cher," Bastien rises and rounds the table faster than he should be able to and gently grasps my arm. Starting beneath his palm, a gentle warmth spreads and envelops me like a cocoon. He nudges me towards him, his green eyes capturing mine, holding my attention until my racing heart slows and I relax. I'm still desperate to get to Seth, but I feel less panicked – more calculating and clearheaded.

"How did you do that?" I breathe.

The corner of his mouth turns up as he tugs me back to sit on the bench. He runs his free hand through his hair and loosens the band holding it back. Sun-kissed waves fall across eyes that seem to smile, exuding a calm that is nearly palpable. In my periphery, Evie turns and walks toward the shack, which I now know is the back side of a much larger cabin. A gentle pressure at my elbow brings my attention back to Bastien.

"A long time ago, *cher*, the Mothers came together and molded the Earth and the *magie élémentaire* – all that elemental power around us - together. It took years and sadly, many of them gave their own lives in the process. But the end result?" He gestures to himself and Auralie. "They made us out of all that energy - seen and unseen. *Tu voi*," he leans in close to me, his voice almost a whisper, "they wanted to protect themselves."

"From vampires?"

"*Oui, ma chère, des vampires et d'autres êtres maléfiques.*" He nods slowly, the corners of his mouth curling upward. "From all evil things."

"Not all vampires are evil," I mumble, dropping my eyes. "Not Seth." My heart lurches when I say his name. Bastien reaches for my other hand, but I pull it away.

"Perhaps," he says, his shoulders dropping as he lets his hand fall.

I am trying to process all this information, but none of it fits together in my head.

"You call them the Mothers. But who are they really? What are they if they can work with magic?"

"A cadre of powerful women who got to the business of using mother nature against herself." He sits back, releasing my hand. "They used their magic to fight fire with fire. Vampire kind are unnatural - but so are the Kretarie - us." He looks up at Auralie, who nods.

Auralie stands over Bastien before sliding onto the bench next to him. "The Mothers, with a little help from the fae, created us to act as a counterbalance."

I don't mean to stare, but what they are telling me is truly crazy. But who am I kidding? Vampires and fae are real, so why is this any stranger? I glance between them, my brow furrowing in confusion.

"They only made two of you?"

Bastien drops his eyes, lets loose a heavy sigh, then looks back at me.

"Once, there were hundreds of us, but the vampires are strong. They organized, and we didn't."

I squirm - the anxiety of inaction getting to me. *Seth always said I was too impatient.* Too much talk and no action.

"Then let's gather the rest of the Kret-" I pause, not sure I remember what they call themselves, "-whoever's left. I only need one of you to come with me. Everyone else can help Auralie and Evie."

Bastien and Auralie share a look, but say nothing.

"What?" I stare at Bastien, waiting for him to agree with me.

He shakes his head, a grim twist to his mouth.

"There's no one to call. We are all that's left."

16
HOLD MY HAND

Octavia

THE MORNING SUN FORCES me awake.

I lay there, thinking about last night. Before I went to sleep, Bastien sat with me and doled out more Kretarie history. He and Auralie have been around since the late nineteen twenties. They were the last two Kretarie created by the Mothers - a coalition of magically gifted humans and fae women.

Funny- most of the things our culture thought were true of vampires apply more to the Kretarie. They don't age, and while the sun doesn't burn them to a crisp, it weakens them significantly.

Each of them has a particular inclination, and Bastien's is emotional energy. That's why his touch calms me down. It's a nice thing to have in a pinch, but it feels... wrong. Seth could always break through my panic, and he's not a badass, magically created Xanax with muscles and wings. He's just my vampire boyfriend and, call me old-fashioned, but I think I prefer that.

I could have slept in the house; Bastien and Auralie gave me my own room, but I spent the rest of the night in the hammock on the porch. I didn't want to be that close to Bastien. I can't let myself get dependent on him and his soothing effect. Not now. But I'm questioning my decision because the sun is finally up and it's *hot*.

"Mornin'!" Bastian calls out the back door.

I give a half-hearted wave. The rough canvas of the hammock is sticking to my sweat-soaked legs which must be covered in mosquito bites the way my skin itches and burns. Daybreak was over an hour ago, but I have just been lying here watching the wind bend the tops of the trees. My anxiety has faded and settled in as background noise.

Maybe I'm giving up? I have been hiding my whole life, and even though I am still hidden now, it feels less like a ticking time bomb. The bayou surrounds me with water, providing a natural barrier I never realized I wanted, and the humidity alone could deter vampires from spending too much time around here. My breath catches.

What if he's not with Illion?

What if he's looking for me?

My heart aches. I'm lounging in a hammock, staring absentmindedly at the trees, while who knows what is happening to him. The thought of this makes my skin crawl. What if he's hurt? What if he's dead?

I scramble out of the hammock, my heart racing. My thoughts rev up and run rampant. Once again, I fall into the worst kind of panic – the kind I can't do anything about. If Seth were here, he would hold me and talk about nonsense. The deep rumble of his voice through his chest would soothe me and take the edge off, but he's not here.

Nausea swells, and the sky spirals in my vision. But before I can spiral out of control, Bastien is there, wrapping one arm around my waist and the other around my shoulders. He pulls me close into a bear hug, and the panic melts away. His breath and heartbeat are slow and deep - hypnotic. We stand there for the longest time until I snap out of it and pull myself back, careful not to let go.

"Thank you," I murmur.

"My pleasure, *cher*," he responds close to my ear.

The way he says that - *cher* - it's like the rustle of silk. Everything he does seems to settle my nerves, which is actually very unnerving. I step back and twist out of the arm he has across my back and put some space between us.

"Why can you do that? You didn't really explain it. You told me what you are, but not how you do what you do." I'm rambling, I know. I sit back down in the hammock with Bastien right in front of me, and I lower my eyes. He drops his arms and crouches, taking one of my hands in his.

"Our kind, like I said before, are made of nothing but energy." The corner of his mouth turns up. "We sense it. Control it." He holds my hand up as his fingers intertwine with mine. He leans sideways to catch my attention and arches one eyebrow. "And your energy is out of control, *cher.*"

I don't speak as he stands, releases me, and heads back inside. I hold my hand up and examine it, as if there will be emotional residue. But it's just my hand so I close my eyes and ease back into the hammock, thinking it might be good to fall back asleep.

I must have, because when I hear rustling fabric and sounds of footsteps - many footsteps - the sunlight on my face is stronger and the cicada song is blaring. I can feel people hovering over me, their whispers not as quiet as they must think they are. The last time I was surrounded like this, it didn't go well, so I fake being asleep like I'm gunning for an Oscar.

"*Est-ce qu'elle dort?*"

"*Oui. Sa force vitale récupère bien.*"

"Stop now! She doesn't understand a word you say." Someone brushes the hair back from my face as more feet shuffle around.

I crack my eyes open. An ancient, tiny slip of a woman with white, unruly tangles leans down near my face, her hand still on the side of my head. She smiles and tucks my hair behind my ear.

"No, but she hears."

It's the same thickly accented voice I remember from the night I arrived. A tall woman steps forward, the others falling in line around her. She stands with authority; her arms crossed in front of her.

"And she remembers." The woman lifts her skirt and kneels beside me, bracelets jangling. "Dat's right, *ma chérie.* You remember me."

I fully open my eyes - there's no point playing dead. Pushing myself up to a sitting position, I survey the small crowd of women around me. I didn't get a chance to really look at them the last time. There are seven of them. The smallest one, the white-haired woman, is smiling brightly at me. I offer her a small one in return before I notice her ears. My mouth drops open.

"You're fae," I breathe.

She smiles, her eyes lighting up like a gleeful child, her youthful behavior surprising me.

"I am." Her eyes sparkle and gleam.

"Leelee, no need for theatrics," the woman kneeling in front of me chides. She turns her attention back to me, rising and offering her hand. "Now, child. It's hot, and we," she nods to the group, "are old. We don't take too kindly to dis heat and humidity."

I stand without accepting her help, which seems to irritate her. She steps back and crosses her arms again, eyeing me.

"Alrighty, alrighty then," she huffs under her breath and lifts her chin. "It's time you come wit' us."

The fae woman named Leelee takes me by the hand and tugs, but I keep my feet planted while the others walk away. Once they are several paces ahead of us, I allow Leelee to guide me down the stairs. As we move away from the porch, the bossy woman stops and looks up at the sky. Her eyes are closed, her chest expanding with a deep breath.

"There's a storm coming, Delphine."

An average-sized woman in jeans and a sweatshirt scans the sky.

"Hurricane, I reckon."

"We had best be going then." The woman turns and pushes past the others. She calls over her shoulder as she rounds the side of the house. "I have questions, and nobody got time to wait on your beauty sleep."

17

LANDMINES

Seth

Darkness surrounds me, a reminder of the predicament I've found myself in. I'm awake now, lying on the floor in a small room. Distant sounds of glass clattering and the pungent smell of rusty iron confirm I am still at Illion's lab.

I push into a sitting position but stop when a fiery pain in my abdomen makes me catch my breath.

"What th-"

Then I remember the port Illion used to force-feed me A-neg blood. With shaking hands, I lift my shirt, bending close to see in the dim light.

It's small, smaller than any of the ports he'd implanted in Tavi, but the skin around the metal is angry and red and warm to the touch.

My first instinct is to rip it out. Even if I bleed to death, it would be better than being Illion's lab rat. My hand curls around the tube, and I steel myself.

"That will only be a minor inconvenience, you do realize."

I didn't notice the dark doorway was cracked open or Illion peering in. The old vampire opens the door wider, allowing more light in the room. Now I can see it is small, like a closet - the metal walls stained a dark color and filthy.

"Thanks for the generous accommodations," I grumble, looking up as I shiver involuntarily. Truth be told, I don't even know where this cell is located. I never saw anything like this during my many visits here, which is most likely why it looks like it hasn't been used in decades. "You spared no expense. Does Arthur approve?"

I can't help but drag my father into the conversation, his name like ash on my tongue. My whole body is shaking, and I grimace, flexing my muscles to try to stop it.

"That would be from the blood loss," Illion offers as my brow furrows. "The shaking. You'll feel better once you feed." He tosses a blood bag at my feet.

"No." When it hits the floor in front of me, I kick it away. The sudden movement sends shockwaves of pain through my body, but I keep my stare fixed on Illion, daring him to come closer.

"Don't be a child. It's type O. It wouldn't do me any good to weaken you to the point of being useless, would it?" He scoffs. "I'm not trying to kill you, boy. I'm trying to understand you."

"Fuck you," I growl, dropping my head as the pain ebbs. I thought I could lure him close enough to grab him, but the pain I just endured from one kick changes my mind. "All the more reason to let myself starve."

Illion sighs, squatting down in front of me.

"She's still alive."

My heart lurches, and I snap my head up.

"I believe the Kretarie have her." Illion arches an eyebrow, a slow smile creeping onto his lips. "You know about Kretarie, don't you?"

Kretarie? My head's a mess right now, but there's not a vampire alive who hasn't heard of Kretarie. Most think they are an urban myth, refusing to believe beings of energy exist. But there are a few of us who know the real story. They are real. They are dangerous. But no one has seen one for decades.

He's probably making it all up to fuck with me.

I shake my head. "They're just an urban legend. They aren't real." I'll play dumb to see where he's going with this.

"They are energy beings, specially created to be the end of vampire-kind. Made by little witchy humans and the fae." Illion tilts his head to the side then taps his temple dramatically. "You know, I believe one of them is a magnif-

icent male specimen — *massive* wings and... everything."
He arches one eyebrow suggestively.

Asshole.

"If I am correct, he's fully capable of manipulating the
emotions of anyone he touches," Illion leans closer, his
eyes glinting, and whispers, "and if my intel is accurate,
he's the one who has her. I wonder what would happen if
she knew the truth about her escape — that you only did
it because your mother *begged* you."

He studies my face, gauging my reaction, but I won't
give him anything. Even though my heart is self-destruct-
ing, it didn't matter how she got away from my brother. I
love her now, and if I know Octavia, nothing will stop her
from doing the stupid thing — trying to find me. That's
the last thing I want. She needs to get as far away from here
as she can.

Illion rises, taking his time to look me over before he
turns and walks out the door, leaving it slightly ajar.

"With that kind of emotional influence, who knows
what ideas he'll put in her pretty little head? If he's smart,
he'll take the opportunity and make her forget about you."
He stops just past the threshold and looks back over his
shoulder. "Or hate you. I'm sure he could do that."

My heart plummets as the door closes, the heavy lock
engaging with a muted click. Before the footsteps fade
away, he calls out, "I'll be back with more. In the mean-

time, eat and rest. You'll need your energy for what's to come."

18

PEOPLE ARE STRANGE

Octavia

THE TINY WHITE-HAIRED WOMAN gives my hand a gentle squeeze.

"My dear," she says, her voice hushed, "best we follow Andra."

The ever-present current of tingling anxiety has begun to slow, but with each step I take, I'm on the edge of spiraling back into heart palpitations. I don't know these people, and I am tired of being passed around to strangers like someone's pet. I want my life the way it was. I want my little house in the East Texas woods. I want to be told to stay inside and stay safe.

I want Seth.

My hands tremble, and my breathing quickens. The wind picks up as we make our way around the side of the house; my vision is swimming as a high pitch whining fills my ears. Spots cloud my eyes when a gentle, warm hand slides onto the back of my neck and a calm rolls over me.

It's Bastien. I turn and see he's got a baseball hat on with an old beach towel thrown across his shoulders despite the suffocating heat. He looks a little ridiculous, but there's concern twisting his face and, to my brain, that makes him safe.

"*Cher*," he says, the look in his eyes apologetic, and I can't help but reach for his hand. Bastien's managed to prove that he wants to help me, though I'm not sure if that's all he wants. Still, the relief is worth the risk. He squeezes the back of my neck, then laces his fingers with mine. Peering over my shoulder, he addresses Leelee.

"I'll take her through the house, Leelee. You go on around. We'll meet you at the front door."

She doesn't protest as Bastien guides me back up the porch stairs. We wind around the hammock stand into the shadowy recesses of the porch where Bastien sheds the hat and towel. As we enter the kitchen, the smells make my stomach growl while Bastien leads me into a living room of sorts and pulls me toward the couch.

"Sit for just a second, Octavia."

I follow, as I seem to do any time he's touching me. It's a bizarre feeling, following Bastien without question. I don't feel controlled, but I feel like the volume in my brain has been turned down. It's like I'm under some strange spell, not concerned at all about Andra anymore.

As I settle on the edge of the sofa, Bastien reaches across me and takes hold of my other hand, gently pulling on my arm to turn me toward him, and I let it happen. His eyes find mine. Surprisingly, it's not weird.

"If you haven't figured it out, those are the Mothers."

A bunch of women traveling in a pack? That makes total sense.

"When I got you back here the other night, Leelee said she had a feeling about you that piqued their interest. That's why they are here now." He leans in closer, his mouth set in a firm line. "I wouldn't let them take you before."

I wouldn't let them take you.

Seth would have said the same thing. Tears blur his face despite the soothing grip of his fingers around mine. The pit in my belly widens. But Seth *did* let them take me. A tear streaks down my cheek. He left me with Evie and trusted I would be fine. I wasn't.

"Why didn't you?"

"The Mothers created me. They have good intentions, but they are powerful women who tend to forget how they affect the people they interact with."

"What do you mean?" My voice lowers, breathy with apprehension.

"They are influential, even when they don't try to be." He seems almost apologetic. "Their entire existence is about intention and manifestation, and when you combine hundreds of years of practice and power, people around them can lose themselves."

Bastien's grip is tighter now, his thumbs rubbing the backs of my hands, his warm skin radiating comfort and safety. His hands are enormous - mine fill his with room to spare, and I find myself staring at them.

"Why are you so concerned about me? You hardly know me."

Bastien glances over his shoulder, presumably toward the front door, his brows furrowed. He shifts his gaze back to me and I'm surprised by the way his eyes search mine. "The moment I picked you up on the roof, I felt something - something important. I've only ever felt that once before when-"

"Bastien!" a Cajun-accented voice calls out. "*Où es-tu?*"

"*Je viens, Séraphine*! I'm coming!" Bastien sighs and stands, pulling me up with him. "I'll explain later, *cher.*"

How am I supposed to go with these women now? Bastien has planted a very large seed of doubt in my mind. I want to grab something in the room and hold on for dear life and it appears that he senses my apprehension.

"Nothing is going to happen to you, Octavia." He offers a hint of a smile. "Just pay attention to what's going on around you. The Mothers can be," he grimaces, "persuasive."

"Great," I mutter as he leads me to the door. When it opens, instead of a gaggle of women, only Leelee waits for me on the porch.

"Off we go," she chirps as she takes me by the elbow, "Come, come."

I follow her down the steps, the gravel crunching under our feet as we head towards a long, dark green SUV, the side door wide open. I turn to see Bastien standing at the top of the step and his words play back.

Just pay attention to what's going on around you. The Mothers can be persuasive.

I don't know what they have in store for me, but whatever it is, I'm the most stubborn person I know. I bite the inside of my lip. I hope that is enough.

19

ASTRONOMICAL

Bastien

THE DUST CLOUD SETTLES as I watch the taillights of the SUV shrink into the shadows of the low-hanging trees. Octavia may be gone, but traces of her aura are everywhere. I flex my hand, whispers of her touch lingering on my palm and twisting through my fingers. I have grown accustomed to the never-ending barrage of emotion constantly surrounding me, so this new taste is sweet.

Intoxicating.

Dangerous.

One hundred years of navigating this sea of energy has taught me to meter what I allow myself to experience, and it has been a long time since I opened my senses to another. It's also given me time to make my peace with the Mothers for choosing this kind of existence for me.

Octavia is an enigma. If I had a lick of sense, I would lock my feelings down tight.

I keep staring down the road, already searching for headlights I know won't be due back for hours. But for what reason, I don't know. There's something about this girl that has me second-guessing myself.

When we got the call to pull her off the Dormande building, I had no idea why, and to be honest, I still don't really know. There's no doubt that was much more than a rescue. I feel it deep down where my sustaining emotion is uncorrupted and pure. It sings louder and brighter than ever when she's close.

But now she's gone, and the silence roars.

20
WAKING UP

Octavia

WE PULL AWAY FROM the house and turn onto a well-worn dirt road. I sit by the window, staring and thinking about everything Bastien said while I do my best to disappear into the vinyl and wood paneling.

My hands rest in my lap, fingers laced taut, knuckles turning white. Old, sprawling trees drip their long branches overhead, keeping us in sweltering shadow most of the time. We drive for at least twenty minutes, rocks continually pinging off the undercarriage. No one speaks the entire time except for Leelee, but she only smiles and coos at me as if I were a baby rabbit she rescued.

All the windows are up, and they don't have the AC on, so I'm dripping with sweat. My skin feels tight and tingly and I remind myself that I should take a shower when I get back. I'm so filthy, even my skin feels wrong.

We arrive at our destination - an antebellum plantation-style mansion that has seen much better days—the peeling paint hints at a butter-yellow history complemented by green and black mold stains under the windows.

The SUV pulls up to the side of the house. Doors slam as the women climb out of the vehicle and file into the house. Leelee opens my door and I slide off the seat onto the gravel drive. The breeze feels good on my skin, but my breaths are coming faster as anxiety rises with no Bastien to quell it. Something makes me feel like I'll never leave if I walk through the door. *Dramatic much, Tavi?*

"Girl," Andra's voice wafts from inside. "You gon' stand outside all day?"

I want to, but I know that's not an option. I give the trees one last look over my shoulder, then take slow strides up the wooden steps to the screen door. It shrieks as I open it, mimicking the sound I'm screaming in my head.

I don't want to do this.

It's dim inside the kitchen, most likely because the windows haven't been washed in decades. Voices carry across the room, but no one is in here and I half-fear that there are actual ghosts in residence. There's an arched door across the room from me, movement casting dancing shadows along the wall.

Andra steps into the doorway and beckons to me.

"In here, Octavia."

I have no other choice but to go. As I walk past her, a little smile tugs at her lips. My stomach churns, my breath catching as I follow her through the doorway and look around the room — the opulence, the mystical aura - totally unexpected in a house so run down on the outside.

Small tapestried sofas and throw pillows are spread around, complemented by low-lit lamps and ornate side tables. High ceilings drip with strings of tiny amber lights. There are no windows, yet the room radiates an other-worldly glow. I feel as if the space has cocooned me in pure wonder.

The Mothers, scattered around the room all attend to different tasks. I notice Leelee first. The tiny woman is settled on a floor cushion with a tray of vials in front of her. Each container is a different size and shape, but all contain the same color liquid. Somehow, her presence gives me relief.

Before I can see what she's doing, Andra is beside me.

"Sit with me." She guides me by the elbow to a pair of worn leather wingback chairs. Settling into our seats, she eyes me with a long, uncomfortable stare. I don't know what to say, so I look down at my hands.

"Octavia, can you describe the treatments you received from Illion?"

"Not really," I mutter, looking up at her through my lashes. I'm surprised they know about Illion, but then I remember Evie and it makes a little more sense. "They hurt. Bad. He said they were to cleanse any trace of my blood from detection after I'd been injured outside of the house."

She purses her lips and frowns.

"Now, *cher*, you are a smart young lady. How is it dat doin' something to the inside of your body? How does it 'cleanse' being sensed from the outside?"

Well, fuck. I had never thought about it. I've been so afraid of detection my entire life, I just went along with what I was told.

"I..." I clear my throat, my mouth dry. "I trusted Seth."

That was all I could offer. If Seth trusted Illion, I trusted Illion. But she's right. I squirm in the chair as I consider what I said and the implications. It doesn't sound so logical now.

Andra leans forward to peer around the side of her chair. Her long, brown and red braids drape against the bracelets covering her forearms, the sound strangely musical. "Manon, you ready?"

"*Oui*," a tall, willowy woman replies. She sets her book on a side table and picks up what looks like a medical bag from the floor. Rounding Andra's chair, she kneels in front of me and smiles. "Just a quick test, *ma chérie.*"

She's pretty, in an older, elegant way. As she tucks her light blonde hair behind her ear, I notice the telltale point. *Another fae.* Manon holds her hand out to me. "May I?"

I assume she means my hand, so reluctantly, I give it to her. With efficiency, she turns my palm up and uses a device to prick the tip of my ring finger, then flips the device over, exposing a paper strip. She touches the paper to the forming droplet, the end turning red as it's absorbed. My pinprick wound disappears simultaneously. I gape at my now unblemished fingertip.

What the actual fuck? I examine my hand.

"Did you see that? Why did my finger do that?"

Manon, watching the digital display, ignores me. She takes a quick breath when it beeps and whirls toward Andra, giving her a look bordering on shock.

"Are you sure?" Andra leans forward, her eyes searching the display, then settling on me.

Manon nods, holding the device out to her. Both women look at one another, the surprise on their faces apparent.

Andra shifts towards me.

"Where are your parents, child?" Andra's tone is softer, less authoritarian.

"Wait a minute!" I hold out my hand, wiggling my finger in shock. "How did you do that?"

She sighs and purses her lips. A few of the other women have joined us, settling themselves on the floor or leaning against Andra's chair. They've all got peculiar looks on their faces, and *they won't stop staring at me*.

It's creepy.

"All in good time, Octavia," Manon says.

Leelee appears beside me, and the feeling of being beneath a magnifying glass recedes. She seems the most reliable, Mother or not. She places one small hand on my arm.

"Your mother and father, Octavia. Where are they?" Leelee asks.

I scan the faces surrounding me. Some are weathered with experience. Some seem barely older than me. But all of them have the same look in their eyes. Bastien's warning echoes in my head, making me choose my words carefully.

"The Directorate took my parents when Cain discovered me. They're probably dead." My voice trembles, the scar in my heart threatening to tear open. My lip quivers, and I have to blink furiously to keep the tears at bay. It never gets easier.

"Why do you want to know?" My voice threatens to break, but I choke out my question before it does.

Manon moves to the side, and Andra takes her place, kneeling in front of me with the device in her hand. "Breathe, child," she whispers, her palm warm against my thigh.

My heart is hammering. *Why are they asking about my parents?*

"What is your earliest memory of them?" Manon asks, her eyes sharp. Her tone is less caring – more analytical. "How old were you?"

I dig back to the earliest thing I can remember. I don't know what they are getting at, but I wish they'd spit it out.

"I remember a lot of things." At least, I think I do. The house. All the different smells in the kitchen. The curtains in my bedroom... How do I figure out which was first?

"You are going to have to be more specific," I tell them. When Manon's eyes narrow with skepticism, I add, "Can *you* remember *your* earliest memory on demand?"

"I am one hundred and three years old. So, no, I cannot."

I'm certain the shock on my face is obvious.

"Ladies," Andra cuts in. "Settle down." She turns to me with a sympathetic smile. "Child, let's try another way. Take me back to grade school. You remember 'dat?"

"I was homeschooled." I shake my head. "I wasn't allowed to go to school, or go out to eat anywhere, or to the park. Nothing." My early childhood memories are one long string of me by myself in an empty house, and most of them are hazy at best.

"Did you have any siblings? A sister, maybe?"

I shake my head. "It was just me."

"She was suppressed," a woman standing behind Andra's chair suggests. She's young with unruly red hair almost contained in a messy bun. She is small, like Leelee, and I think I see the tip of a pointed ear peeking out from escaped curls. Several other women nod in agreement.

"It should be wearing off by now," Manon offers, looking to Andra for approval. "We won't need to get around anything once she's clear."

"Hold on." I stand and elbow my way out of whatever secret circle meeting they have going on. "No one's 'getting around' anything in my head. Not until someone explains this!" I present my hand, finger outstretched, trying to look as demanding as I can.

Manon is the first to respond.

"Do you take some sort of medication every day?"

I nod. At home there were the vitamins my mother was fanatical about, and since I escaped the Directorate, it has been a daily maintenance medication courtesy of Illion to help keep me hidden.

"Have you taken anything since you arrived in the bayou?"

I bristle, crossing my arms over my chest. "No. I didn't exactly pack for a trip."

Andra stands, pulling something from one of the deep pockets in her voluminous dress. She moves fast, and before I know it, she's taking my hand and drawing a small knife across my palm. The pain isn't terrible, but her sudden assault is a shock.

"What the hell!" I yank my hand back and cradle it with the other. Leelee scurries to me, pressing a piece of cloth against my palm and clucking to herself in a maternal sort of way.

"It's alright," she says with a hopeful smile before she pulls the cloth back. "See?"

I inspect my hand to find an angry red welt where the knife was drawn. A thin sheen of blood is already drying, but there is no cut. Even the redness is beginning to fade. A memory flashes through my mind of Seth and I in the kitchen making dinner. He cut his thumb with a paring knife, and I freaked out. He just laughed and held it up for me to see that the wound had already closed on its own.

One of the few vampire benefits.

That's what he told me.

That would mean...

No.

Not possible.

"No." It comes out as a whisper.

"Yes, *enfant*. You've got the vampire blood in you." Andra says. "You aren't A negative, Octavia. That's not why they were hiding you. You are one-of-a-kind—a blend of something impossible."

"What makes me impossible?" I stand. My nerves are in overdrive, and I'm ready to run. "What are you saying?"

Manon hands Leelee the testing device and she holds it up for me to look the display.

I cannot process what I am seeing. The digital readout is flashing an error symbol, but the words beneath it read

Vamylkan

Feyilkan

21

EVEN IF IT HURTS

Genevive

Lying on the chaise in the middle of the room with a rope around my abdomen is not where I expected to wake up. I try to sit, but my bindings keep me prone. It has only been half an hour or so since Arthur's henchmen dragged me in here, and I am starting to wonder if my husband decided I wasn't worth his time.

Twisting my neck, I look back towards the section of my closet where my coats hang and notice a gap where two have been pushed aside. A smile threatens to show itself, but I hold it back to keep from giving my discovery away. The door to my room opens, and I let my neck relax.

"Really, Arthur?" I almost chuckle as I say it.

My husband, the Grand Master Arthur Dormande, leans against the doorframe, studying me rather than responding. Lifting my head to get a better look at him, I blow out a breath and purse my lips disapprovingly.

"I expected something more diabolical than my closet." I sigh and shift my gaze to the ceiling. "I don't know what you are playing at Arthur, but it won't work."

He pushes away from the door and saunters toward me, his steps slow and intentional. He stops at the single arm of the velvet lounge sofa and brushes one hand over the fabric. "It smells like her."

I can't help but roll my eyes. "Of course, it does. She was sitting there."

"What about all the others? Did you hide them in here too?"

Here we go.

I've played this scene over in my head since we were married. I even practiced what I would say and how I would say it, but I abandon my well-rehearsed plan. I've decided the best course of action is to call his bluff and not hold anything back.

All these years, I kept my activities and my son's condition secret, and now that I am shining a light on both, it feels like watching a kite fly away. I kept working against his elitest views in the shadows, and I accomplished much of what I set out to do. There's nothing to lose by being honest now. Arthur has Seth. He knows about his inability to digest A-negative blood. He is unraveling what I have been up to as well. Pretending or deflecting has no value in this conversation now.

"You obviously know about Seth's condition, but why do you care? You have Cain. He's your favorite anyway."

My husband's glare bores into me. Even with all bets off, his expression shakes me. Years of practice has steeled me, but I've never been in this position before, so fear slides in and takes the place of confidence. He is a powerful, unscrupulous man who would enjoy every minute of breaking me. With Seth exposed, and my extracurricular activities revealed, I am of no use to him anymore. Unless I can find one iota of leverage, my time might finally be up.

"You and your family name were my ticket to raise myself and my rescue efforts above the scrutiny of the Directorate."

His nostrils flare with annoyance.

"People seldom look up to find traitors," I add with as much snark as I can muster.

"Comedy? Genevive, I didn't think you had a sense of humor." Arthur folds his arms over his chest, tilting his head as he scrutinizes me. "This is not a joke and I don't buy your little devil-may-care act."

I meet his eyes with a glare of my own, then snort to myself. Arthur is all brawn and no brain. Like Capone, he did one thing exceptionally well: kill. Aside from that, he had the thought process of a middle school boy. The only smart thing he ever did was surround himself with intelligent advisors.

"I'm not asking you to buy anything, Arthur." No reason to draw this out. All I can do now is try to help Seth, though I have to face the reality that it may be too late.

I'm dead already.

Arthur shakes his, head pacing a slow circle around me. "You didn't think your little stories through, love."

My eyes widen; my confusion is apparent and Arthur can't help but smile.

"I know you *think* you've saved the masses." He stops in front of me and leans in close. "But you couldn't even save your precious little sickling child, could you?"

I swallow hard. What happened to all the humans I tried to help?

He straightens up, a smug expression settling on his face.

"You're wondering about your little A-neg underground railroad now, aren't you?"

My breath catches.

"I must admit, I thought about choking off that flow of blood from the get-go, but Illion talked some sense into me."

"Il-Illion?" My voice cracks as the gravity of Arthur's words register.

"My mastermind, my love."

The faces of so many humans flash in my head, each one fully trusting in my ability to save them from collection. My chest aches as I think of them all. Men, women, *children...*

"The Directorate is grateful for your clever plan of funneling in more food sources. So grateful, I believe, we must celebrate you publicly." Arthur opens his arms wide and laughs. "The Trickster Huntress of the Directorate!"

I clutch at my dress, my vision swimming. He's going to tell the world I deceived all those people - that I tricked them into revealing themselves. Years and years of painstaking planning - all the dangerous initiatives carried out under my command - twisted to make me a vampiric demon when all I wanted was redemption.

"No..." I whisper, my voice trembling, "Arthur, *please.*"

"What's this? The unflappable Genevive Dormande begs?" Arthur, clearly enjoying himself, parades around my closet as if on a stage. "Let me see if I have the story right."

He sits on the edge of the chaise by my feet, too lost in the glee of dismantling me piece by piece.

"You asked Seth to play his role, and because you were helping to harbor his girlfriend, he, in exchange, fulfilled his role in the Council." He sighs in disappointment. "Vivi, didn't you realize that someone would have noticed Seth's continual disappearing act?"

"Seth has no friends here. He has no love for this place," I murmur. "Unlike his selfish, narcissistic, dangerous brother who relishes the power this family holds." My eyes lock with his, my voice finding strength I didn't know I had. "Just like you."

"All this time, I thought you were smarter than this." Arthur shakes his head, unaffected by my slight.

"I'm smart, and you know it - unlike my idiot best friend!" I hiss. *I have to throw him off, and Anna is his kryptonite.*

"Don't," Arthur warns, his voice low as his fists ball at his sides. "I will not allow you to speak of Annabella in that manner. She was -"

"A *fool*. Your power blinded her. She was so subservient to your demands she lost herself. If she had resisted you one iota, you would not feel the same way. You only love what you can control."

A stinging slap turns my face away from Arthur, ending my part in the conversation. He stands over me, his anger unmistakable.

"The only thing stopping me from killing you is the mess I'd have to deal with. I will keep you alive, but," he sneers, his breath wafting across my face, "only until the world hears of your *humanitarian* exploits."

I close my eyes and say a silent prayer for my son.

I'm done. It's over.

22

HERE COME THE MONSTERS

Seth

I CAN'T LIFT MY head. I have no muscle control because I am so damn weak, sitting on the floor in a dark room, propped against the wall. There are too many shadows and in this position, my eyes can only see the floor.

I am not sure if it is the same cell as before, but I don't think it is because it smells less... rusty. It's quiet, except for the occasional beep and whir from outside the door. That means he has moved me closer to his lab. Cold fear takes root in my chest.

"How are we feeling, Seth?" Illion's voice fills the quiet space.

I attempt to raise my head, my chin coming to rest on my chest. I feel a tiny rivulet of drool running from the corner of my mouth, dribbling onto my t-shirt. I grunt with the strain of trying to lift my hand. *Why can't I move?*

"Poor boy," Illion drawls, feigning concern. "Your energy is low. I know, I know."

"Wh-what...are... you doing t-to me?" My voice escapes in a ragged rasp. I can't even lift my head to face the bastard. If I could move, I'd rip his throat out, but I can't even wipe my own mouth. This uselessness makes my blood boil.

"What do you think I am doing? I am experimenting, boy."

The boil overflows into sheer rage.

"For what?" I spit my words like venom. "Why?"

"Settle down," Illion coos at my outburst. "Remember, I need you healthy *and alive* if I want to continue my testing."

"Testing?" My breathing is ragged and my brow drips with stinging condensation as my chest heaves.

"My boy, I need to know why you can stomach all other blood types. If I can find out what makes you special, it will open so many avenues for our kind. So many..." his voice trails off, a smile warping his face. "Your father will give me anything I want. Any lab. Any test subject. Anything. I. Want."

"Octavia," I murmur, and I ache at the sound of her name

Spots form in what little vision I have left as I lean to the side, my eyelids fluttering. "What di-did... you do w-with... Octavia?"

Illion sighs and unlocks the door. As he kneels beside me, he pulls a vial from his pocket.

Not again.

My eyes widen at the sight of the blood-filled tube.

"Don't worry, boy. This is the kind you can drink." He holds the vial up in front of me. "It's O negative. Fresh."

My mouth waters at the sight despite the disgust and anger I feel brimming inside of me. I don't want to need what he has, but even if I did, I cannot lift my hand to take the vial from him.

"Let me help." Illion pops the rubber stopper and holds the delicate glass to my lips. He cradles my head back as I devour the contents, my sense of self-worth disappearing as quickly as the blood drains down my throat.

Licking the final drops off my lips, my strength returns enough for me to lift my head higher and glare at the older vampire. A warm sensation takes hold in my belly and spreads throughout my limbs. I feel like my body is waking from a long hibernation.

"Where is Octavia, Illion?" My voice is a low growl, stronger and surer than before.

"I told you." He raises an eyebrow and shakes his head. "But I already have all the information I need from her, so I don't really care. You made sure of that every time you brought her here."

Every time I brought her here. The blood I just ingested threatens to come back up. How could I have been so *stupid?*

Illion stands, his tall, lanky frame towering over me. "When your father said I could take you, I refused to waste time." He inclines his head, changing his tone to a conspiratorial whisper. "I was afraid he'd change his mind if I stuck around any longer."

"Does he have her?" My voice cracks. I know he told me something about some kind of creature, but I don't trust him. "Tell me the truth."

Illion frowns, then laughs.

"Are you daft from weakness?" He stands and brushes his hands on his coat. "I told you, the Kretarie has her." He turns back to the door, resting one hand on the frame. "I would stop thinking about her, son."

"Don't call me that." My fists ball at my sides, anger threatening to sweep me into a rage I have never felt before. I pull my legs underneath me, shifting to my feet, not breaking eye contact with Illion.

With a burst of energy I do not understand, I lunge. I want to rip my arms out of their sockets just to get to Illion sooner. A giant is roaring inside of me, and I can't control it. The chains around my wrists do it for me.

"Oh," he says, unfazed by my sudden movement. "My additive seems to be working." The fascination creeping onto his face is nothing short of diabolical.

"What have you done?" I scream, frantically tugging against my chains. "What are you doing to me?"

The words explode out of my mouth before I crumple to the floor in a sobbing heap, curling into myself. My skin burns from the inside, and there is a buzzing behind my eyes like wasps trapped in a glass jar. Illion watches me the way one watches a wounded animal on the side of the road, intrigued but not invested enough to do anything about it. He frowns as my screams become wails and moans, sighing as he steps out of the room, leaving me in the dim light of a single light bulb.

I weep like a child. It makes me sick to hear myself, but everything *hurts*. More than my body, more than my hunger, my soul aches for Octavia. *My Tavi*. I'm terrified she's lost to me, so why should I fight any of this? Why did I think taking her to my mother was a good idea?

On the floor, my face is pressed against the cold tiles, sweat and tears burning streaks down my face, forming a puddle around me. If my father has her, she's done for. But if the Kretarie has her, I don't even know how to feel. Maybe she's safe?

I pray she is. I plead to whatever god kind enough to listen to keep her from doing what I know she will.

"Don't come for me," I whisper as I close my eyes.

"Wh-here a-am I?"

I startle at the sound of another voice. My eyelids grate against the delicate tissue of my eyes as I struggle to open them. The light is dim, but I can still see, even with my face pressed to the ground. I lift my head.

A frail young man sits in the corner; his worried eyes fixed on me. His feet are bare, and a thin hospital gown hangs from his narrow shoulders. There are numbers stamped on the fabric.

1-4-3

My heartbeat quickens, speeding up as if I just hit an accelerator. More conscious now, I sit up. There's a strange tang in the air, metal-like but it's almost sweet. Saliva pools at the corner of my mouth, and I wipe it with the back of my hand, but I freeze when I look at my wrist.

No chains.

I lift my eyes back to the man.

"Who are y-ou?" The young man has pulled his knees up to his chest and is shaking so hard I can see it from across the cell. I can *feel* it. He's like a bird, the way his heart flutters and thrums. "Did you sign up for the trials too?" He whispers, peering wide-eyed around the shadowy cell.

Wh-?

My eyes zero in on rivulets of blood dripping down both of his arms. Without even thinking, my fangs descend.

"Dinner is served." Illion's voice drifts across the room from a speaker mounted in the corner, my body going stiff at the sound. "Let's see how hungry you are."

Since my birth, I have only directly fed from a human once, and it took the majority of my adolescent life to bury the trauma it caused. Cain bullied me into it, and I regret it to this day. Since then, with the help of my mother, I learned to block my instincts and hold my vampiric need at bay. But right now, I cannot control the need coursing through my body. My heart plummets as my senses roar to life. Before I can stop myself, I launch across the cell and latch greedily onto the man's arm like an animal. My victim can only whimper as he slides down to the floor.

He is too weak to fight.

I am too weak to resist. It only takes a minute or two before I hear a hitch and stutter, his heart finally quiet.

What have I done?

My body sings with new life while the one beneath me flutters away.

What have I done?

Horror envelops me and steals my breath. If the blood didn't fuel me or taste like heaven, I would retch until I purged myself of this monstrous thing I have done, but I can't bring myself to. All I can do is lay this poor man's head down and help him close his eyes before I retreat to the opposite corner and cower like the animal I am becoming.

23

TORN

Octavia

My brain is mush, but an energy I can't explain sings in my blood. The Mothers made a fuss, their voices ricocheting in my head and becoming a tangled mess. I don't remember a word they said.

I'm curled up on the couch inside Bastien's house, trying to persuade the enormous pillows to swallow me whole. Bastien perches on the edge of the coffee table. He's been sitting beside me for the better part of an hour, worry lines creasing his brow. He squeezes my hand, giving me a nudge of soothing energy, and my fingers curl into his. *He's just trying to help*, I reason with myself, trying and counter how much I seem to enjoy his touch.

"Look at the bright side," a sly smile curls up one corner of his mouth, "you aren't A negative. Hell, you aren't even human, which takes you off the entire vampire menu."

I don't say anything. Instead, I focus on the window behind him and try to pretend everything is normal.

Bastien's other hand closes over mine. "You're awfully quiet, *cher*."

"I'm thinking about my new identity." The snark drips from my tongue. I flinch and regret my tone before the words have even left my mouth. He is sitting across from me with actual concern in his eyes, and I'm being a jerk.

Bastien smiles anyway, and my heart flutters until I put that part of my brain on lockdown. *Think of Seth* - his smell, the feel of his hands, the sound of his voice. He's out there, probably hurting, and I'm lounging on someone's couch.

My heart drops as nightmares of Seth in pain ricochet through my mind. I squeeze my eyes closed against the onslaught. I've been trying to keep these intrusive thoughts at bay, distracting myself with my newfound heritage, but once I let my mind invent images like that, it's like a dam has broken.

Warmth floods through my body.

My eyes snap to Bastien.

"I'm sorry, *cher*, but you might as well be yelling out loud."

I know his intentions are honorable, but it's beginning to feel like he's stalking me. I want to pull my hand from his grasp, but it's getting harder and harder to will myself to move away.

"If I need your help, I'll ask," I snap, flustered.

He frowns, and I instantly regret my words. The warmth retreats as he lets go, pushing away from the couch to stand.

"Fair enough," he mumbles, then takes a breath. "Look at the bright side. With you off the menu, it means your boyfriend will really have an easier time being with you."

"Seth loves me. *That's* why he has an easy time."

"I didn't mean anything by it." Bastien shakes his head and looks away. "I was just thinking logically."

I close my eyes. He's right, and I hate that he's right. My stomach churns. What if Bastien is just a really good guy, and he is only trying to help me? Given all the touchy-feely stuff, that seems unlikely, but that's not what I should be concerned about. I love Seth, and nothing, *no one*, will change that. I sit up on my elbows and narrow my eyes.

"Okay, then, if I'm off the menu and out of vampire territory, why am I hiding?"

"Lots of reasons, *cher*." Bastien lights up like a child in a candy store with money to burn. "Let's start with the fact that you are something that shouldn't exist. Powerful people crave rare things, whether they need them or not. And you are the rarest of rare."

I don't know what to say to that, and I really don't understand his excitement, either. I'm in a full-blown overdose of life-altering information, and I have hit critical mass. All I can do is stare.

The silence holds for a moment, then we're both startled as Auralie strides out of the kitchen, brushing her hands off after popping a piece of fruit in her mouth.

"Which is valuable to practically everyone," she says as she chews. She stops at the end of the couch and sits on the arm, watching me expectantly.

"I shouldn't exist?"

"Not in anyone's wildest dreams," she says, brushing her hands on her thighs. "I honestly think you are a medical impossibility."

Wow. Way to make a girl feel special.

Pushing up to sit, I swing my legs over the edge of the couch, then angle myself to face both of them.

"I get that my blood shouldn't draw attention. Vampires shouldn't be on to me every time I bleed, yet they are." I stand. "Every time I got a cut - a scratch, even - we rushed to Illion so I could get one of his treatments. What was all the theater about if my blood is not what they want?"

"There's a multitude of reasons," Auralie says. "One, you terrify them, so they want to keep tabs on you." She stands and starts to pace. "Two, it was a story concocted to keep you docile and willing to play their game. Your vampire boyfriend had to do something to keep you under control."

"Control?" My voice shoots out a little louder than I intend. My fists are clenched at my sides because she's gone too far. "Seth was *protecting* me."

"Protecting, hiding, controlling... whatever," Auralie mumbles, her hand swatting the implication aside. "Bottom line: the vampires are afraid of you. Fear and desire are first cousins, didn't you know?" With one of her eyebrows arched, she throws me a look. "Use your brain, girl."

Auralie shakes her head and then disappears into the kitchen, returning with an apple before heading out the front door. Before she leaves, she shoots Bastien a warning glance. "Leave this explanation to the Mothers, Bas."

A heavy silence envelopes the room. Shifting on my feet, I steal a quick glance at Bastien, but I'm not quick enough. His hazel eyes lock on mine, and my stomach flutters. He stands and approaches me slowly like I'm a stray animal waiting to bolt if given a chance.

"Auralie can be, ah..." he runs a hand through his hair, "hard to take sometimes."

His scent is strong - almost overpowering - but something about it makes me want to breathe more deeply. My head only reaches his shoulder, the crook beckoning me to lean into the warmth he radiates. My pulse quickens, my weight rocks back on my heels, and his expression softens.

Shit. He can tell.

"It's okay, cher," he consoles me as he reaches for my hand again, mistaking my reaction for fear. "Nothing to be afraid of."

I chuckle, nervous energy radiating off me.

"I'm not afraid," I mumble, looking down at my feet, at the floor... at anything but him. My cheeks flush, my body humming for more.

He tightens his hold on my hand, his thumb brushing back and forth across my knuckles. Warmth spreads through my arm and washes over my body. My eyes shutter closed.

"Stop it," I whisper.

His thumb stops moving, but his grip stays the same. The warm sensation retreats down my arm, and I let out a shaky breath.

"Octavia."

His voice is low.

I shift to face him, leaving my eyes cast down. This is becoming uncomfortable, but not in a threatening way. Shame borders on guilt because I've discovered that I like...no, I want Bastien's attention.

Think about Seth.

"Remember, the Mothers made me from energy, and I am made..." he begins, his voice as gentle as his touch as he lifts our locked hands, "mostly from human energy, *emotional* energy."

I risk peeking up at his face. I've heard of people smiling with their eyes, but Bastien's literally oozes kindness. He has a strong, defined jawline with cheekbones for days, but those hazel eyes soften his countenance. Bastien has rescued me, taken care of me, and tried to keep me from completely losing my shit. All signs point to Bastien being safe, which makes me want to trust him, but that still goes against every instinct I have.

"Maybe I don't want you to change how I feel." My voice lacks conviction. I don't even believe me.

"It's not a choice. It's who I am."

My breath catches before I let out a groan. That *smile*. I'm caught up in it and don't protest when he releases my hand and tucks my hair behind my ear. But in that one motion, Bastien unknowingly calls up memories of Seth, and my heart lurches.

What am I doing? My stomach lurches.

"I'm gonna be sick," I croak as I bolt and run for the kitchen.

Seth is being held by someone capable of unspeakable things, and I'm flirting with my emotionally charged, vampire-killing rescuer. Chills seep into my bones. I'm a horrible person.

Gripping the edge of the sink, I breathe deeply. The last thing I need is Bastien feeling the need to "help" me.

I'm losing sight of my priorities - Seth being the most important - and I need to get it together. Now that I know my blood won't summon the masses, I have no reason to hide while Seth suffers.

"I'm going after Seth," I say, loud enough for him to hear in the other room. Creaking footsteps tell me he's following.

Why can't he leave me alone? It's my death wish, not his.

"No one's gonna die, death wish or not."

"What th-" I whirl around, my chest tight.

He taps his temple, a smirk playing on his lips. "I can do that too, remember?"

"No." *Shit!* The blood drains from my face. "A lot's happened since I got here."

"*Écoutez, cher.* Listen to me. Your boy can hold his own. Besides, how will you break him out by yourself?" He crosses his arms in front of his chest, arching one eyebrow.

Now he's done it. Reassure me, tempt me, even anger me, and you might make me see your point. But question my ability to do something? *Big* mistake, Bastien.

Time to pivot.

"You're right," I frown, then shake my head. "I'm being rash. Seth's strong. He can handle Illion."

"He's tough, yes?" Bastien 's gives me an encouraging nod. He's either eating it up or he's a better actor than I am.

"Yes," I lie, my palms clammy. Honestly, he's more of a diplomat than a tough guy. *Can he survive Illion?* I bite my lip, my eyes hot. *He doesn't have a choice. He* has *to.*

Bastien gestures to the back patio. "I've got to get dinner started. Come sit with me."

I nod, a small smile lifting my lips. I'll sit. I'll smile. I'll do everything he expects of the shaken girl that shouldn't exist. But rest assured, I will be gone as soon as I figure a way out of here.

24

FIGURE YOU OUT

Bastien

'She's going to try and run.'

I make quick eye contact with Auralie over the dinner table. She acknowledges my message but returns to her bowl as if it's her mission to shovel as much gumbo into her mouth as she can. It never ceases to amaze me how much she appreciates food; our kind don't need it.

The sky outside the kitchen window flashes, and a low, rolling thunderclap rattles the glass. The approaching storm forced us inside. I glance over my shoulder at the television in the living room, where whatever show was playing has been interrupted by the local news channel. We'll be staying inside for a while by the looks of the radar. While no one wants a hurricane in these parts, it might be just the thing we need to keep Octavia here, though the timing is peculiar. Hurricane season is long over.

Auralie follows my eyes and smirks. Chuckling to herself, she takes another giant bite of food.

'I'd like to see her try.'

Auralie smirks and shakes her head as she chews. I think she underestimates Octavia, but I'm not making that mistake.

"Should we be doing anything? Boarding up windows or something?" Octavia casts a nervous glance at the window as a strong gust slams the intensifying rain against the glass. She's sitting forward in her chair; heel is bouncing like crazy as a short round of lightning bursts matching the speed of her knee. Looking back at me, her hazel eyes completely conflict with the worry she's attempting to convey.

She's trying hard to appear rattled, but her energy says otherwise. It's unmistakable; a constant wash of color and electricity that undulates around her. On the surface, it is a messy tangle of confusion and uncertainty, none of which has any direction. But at her core, the knowledge that she was lied to, that she isn't a coveted blood vintage, has made room for dangerous new emotions — recklessness and rage.

"Nah, *cher,* it'll take more than a storm to hurt this ol' house." I smile, trying to soothe her into relaxing the death grip she has on her spoon, but she's not listening to me. "Just a little *ouragan* is all."

Auralie pushes away from the table and turns, dropping her bowl in the sink.

"I gotta check on the Mothers," she says with a noisy burp, brushing her hands down her trousers. "They're so absent-minded, they've probably got half the windows open in that old house of theirs."

I nod without breaking eye contact with Octavia. She's a spring wound tight, and I don't think she knows how close she is to exploding.

"*Bon Dieu!*" Auralie mutters after a few seconds of silence and rolls her eyes. "Y'all got *beaucoup* tension up in here. I gotta be on my way." She makes a beeline for the back door, letting the wind slam it shut behind her as she leaves.

Octavia keeps her eyes fixed on me, and while I am transfixed, she is contemplating the fastest route out of here. The wind howls outside. Trees creak all around the house, small branches and twigs clattering on the tin roof. Finally, after another gust of wind slaps rain against the side of the house, she blinks.

"It doesn't sound like just a..." she searches for the word, but gives up and shakes her head, "...whatever you called it." She sets her spoon down, the muscles in her jaw working as she glares at me. The lights above the table reflect in her eyes; they're sharp, thousands of little daggers poised to lash out. She takes a breath, then blows it out.

I know she has more to say, so I wait, exuding a calm energy wave from my center to settle the vibrations in the air into a comfortable purr. She's been resistant to my help, but I'm only adjusting the atmosphere in the room this time. I study the slight movements in her expression as the tension begins to melt. *There, now.* No harm, no foul.

"Why isn't anyone listening to me?" Her words are quiet; her voice is hoarse. "You all act like it's just another day. Meanwhile, my life is falling apart."

Desperation creeps into her tone — I can feel it rolling off her the way I can sense the storm building outside. My hand reaches for hers instinctively, but she drops her eyes and inches back in her chair.

Away from me.

"Ah, *cher*, you're right." I rise and pick up our bowls. Then, slowly, deliberately, I run the faucet and rinse them, giving her time to see that I'm not trying to manipulate her. I only want to help, but I am beginning to fear she'll never see it that way. "I'll get some linens for the guest room so you can get some rest. Tomorrow, we'll make a plan, yeah?"

"*Tomorrow?*"

I startle at her tone, finding her standing, fists balled at her side. The fierce, angry energy she's throwing makes me catch my breath. Her defiant glare burns, and I swear I can hear her heartbeat thrumming like a cornered deer. The wind and rain outside increase with her agitation. It might be worth a call to Leelee, seeing as how this storm and Octavia's temper doesn't seem to be diminishing.

"Octavia." I hold my hands up and take a step in her direction. "There's a hell of a storm coming in, and it's already dark."

"You flew me off that roof in Houston in a storm. *Try again*."

Merde! How do I navigate this without setting her off more?

"You're right; I did. But I don't know where we'd be going, and unless you have some magic GPS in that pretty head of yours, I don't think you could point me in the right direction." Her brow furrows, and I know she knows I'm right. But she's not going to admit it, and that's okay. Dark circles under her eyes and the way her shoulders sag tell me she's exhausted and overwhelmed.

I am about to suggest she wash up while I get the extra room ready, but her bottom lip begins to quiver, and that's all it takes. Before I can blink, she's in my arms, and I pour out as much safety and calm as I can, trying to buy her some peace. My cheek presses against the top of her head as she leans into me, and I have to catch myself before I let her presence consume me.

Her need for balance pulls at my very being, and I cannot resist her, my arms banding tighter around her. The Mothers created me to be their sword and shield, but Octavia requires something different, something *more*, and I am ready.

It's been a very long time since I've used my abilities to shield and protect. I wasn't made for safety; my purpose has always been defense, but the two go hand in hand. I have to keep myself in check, or I fear I will allow the sword to show itself because I am angry she's been hurt. If she weren't depending on me to be here right now, no vampire would be safe. None would escape my wrath. Especially one named Arthur Dormande.

Eyes closed, I inhale her scent, then carefully sift through the chaos and feel for her fear. It hides within a deceptive shell of uncertainty. She has no direction, no anchor, free-falling through lost identity and strange new realities. Everything she knows has been stripped away; by strangers, no less. Taking a chance, I try to nudge a sliver of resolve into her core. It's a tricky thing, and I am out of practice, but I manage to get it done. Her response is immediate.

"I'm okay," she murmurs against my shirt, pulling away. "I mean, you did that, right?"

Not wanting to admit it, I try to play it down as I untangle myself from all the energy swirling around her.

"Nah, *cher*," I grin as I step backwards toward the laundry room, "I just try to keep things smooth, y'know? You do all the hard work yourself." The linen closet door creaks as I begin pulling out sheets and a blanket while I put some needed distance between us and gain control of myself.

"Well, thank you." She reaches for the linens, avoiding eye contact. "You made me feel better."

"I can't make feelings, I just control the volume, *tu vois*?" With a gesture, I show her the way down the hall. "Second door on the left."

"Really," she says just before disappearing down the hallway, "thank you."

25

YOU GOTTA RUN

Octavia

THE RAIN HASN'T LET up, though now and then there's a brief lull punctuated by rolling thunder and near-constant flashes of lightning. I can't help but think it's a perfect time to make a break for Illion's, with all the rain to shield me. The digital alarm clock on the nightstand blares 1:00 A.M., the blue light is bright but still a pale comparison to the storm.

Every time I close my eyes, all I see is Seth. I see how he looked at me when I woke up at Illion's. I feel how he kissed me in the car as we drove to Houston. I ache for the protective hold his arms had on me when we arrived at his mother's.

He's somewhere out there, suffering more than I could possibly imagine, and I am lying in a strange being's guest bedroom somewhere in the backwater bayou eating gumbo and communing with crazy old ladies. My heart aches, and the pit in my stomach deepens.

Bastien said he would help me. Do I believe him? He calms my screaming anxiety and seems to want to help. I think want him to, but... I throw an arm over my eyes. There's something about the way he looks at me that makes me second-guess myself. He did save me, I can't deny that, and the way he held me tonight made me feel safer than I have ever felt, but it also made me feel wrong in so many ways.

Thunder breaks again, the warning flash happening nearly simultaneously. I curl up under the quilt and squeeze my eyes shut, willing myself to sleep. But just as my eyes begin to feel heavy, the hinges on the door creak. I hold my breath, ready to yell for Bastien until a small voice I recognize whispers my name.

"Octavia?" The voice is almost lost to the storm. Leelee slides into the room and closes the door behind her, careful not to let the lock click too loud. Her movements are careful, as if she is trying to be sneaky even though I am already awake.

"I thought you were asleep," she says in a normal voice. "I didn't want to frighten you."

"What are you doing here?"

Her hair is damp, and when I peer over the edge of the bed, I see bare feet and the bottom of her pants soaked through. She holds her hand out to me, worry lines creasing her brow as she glances over her shoulder.

"You have to come with me."

"Now?" The rain is still steady, the storm raging with no signs of stopping. "Where?"

I don't know why, but the urgency in her tone hits, so I scramble out of bed and start slipping on my jeans. I've almost got my shoelaces tied when the door opens again. I freeze and lift my head. It's Bastien.

"We've gotta go. Now." The words were an order, clipped and hard, not a request.

My breath catches. This is not the blue jeans and t-shirt wearing, gently oozing safety and peace Bastien I clung to in the kitchen. This Bastien is covered head-to-toe in black, and if looks could kill, his would incinerate. *This is the custom-made weapon to destroy the vampires.* Dark shadows and milky blue light fall across his face, accentuating his angled features and nearly turning him to stone. His jaw works, his muscles twitching anxiously while he waits for me to finish and stand.

"You going by way of Barataria?" he says to Leelee as we brush past him.

"What is going on?" I stop in the doorway, my hand still in Leelee's as she forcefully tugs me to continue. "It's the middle of the night and storming. Bastien,"

I place one hand on his arm, recoiling as energy like a hot wind roars through my body. He levels his eyes on me, and I swear all the colors are swirling, angrily writhing and waiting to strike.

Lightning flashes, illuminating his wings in an ominous silhouette. They are no longer tightly tucked behind him and, between the storm and the shadows in the house, he looks different, almost sinister. But there's a strange sense of safety alongside the uncharacteristic darkness, and I can't take my eyes off him. The hairs on the back of my neck rise, but a tug on my hand brings me back to my senses.

"Octavia, Bastien is taking you to a place called Briarwood." Leelee starts moving down the hall with me in tow. She glances back. "Yes, I will use Barataria." She frowns as she gives me a quick once-over. "I'd try to take her with me, but I don't know how she'll travel as a half-blood."

"What—" I start, my jaw snapping shut as I glance between the two of them. Even Leelee is different — less delicate and more resolute. "What happened to making a plan in the morning?"

All I have been asking for, pleading for, is someone to have the same sense of urgency as me, but now that it is happening, I'm questioning it. *What's wrong with me?*

Leelee drops my hand and gestures to Bastien. When I turn to face him, I hear the kitchen door slam shut as Leelee leaves. Headlights reflect off a mirror on the wall while gravel crunches as she pulls away from the house, leaving the two of us alone amidst the chaos. Bastien runs a hand through his hair and takes me by the elbow, guiding me to the kitchen. He's moving fast, and I nearly stumble trying to match his pace.

"I don't have time to explain, but the Mothers had a..." he sighs, "disagreement tonight, and Leelee needs to get you out of here before Andra shows up. When they have a disagreement, I usually side with Leelee, but it's *bad* bad to be on the wrong side of Andra. Best we vacate long enough for her to cool her heels and give them all a chance to come to an agreement."

He pulls a worn leather jacket off the hook on the back of the door and hands it to me. "Put this on."

I must hesitate too long because Bastien drapes the jacket over my shoulders and guides my arms through the oversized sleeves. I watch his face, unable to tear my eyes away.

He's not telling me everything.

But the way he gently pulls the zipper up beneath my chin, careful to tuck my hair away from the silver teeth, is a contrast to his darkly focused self. His eyes dart from me to the windows with every crack of thunder, and I can see he's thinking. *Hard.* He definitely knows something that he's not saying.

"I'm fine," I say as I adjust the collar, careful to avoid touching his hands. "I don't mind getting a little wet. The car's not that far."

The corner of his mouth turns up.

"We're not driving." His wings twitch and shift. "But don't worry, *cher*," he says as he reaches around me to open the back door, the wind stealing whatever words he was trying to say.

Wind whips my hair across my face, spraying me with a fine mist of rain and making my skin itch. I raise my hand to my cheek and wipe the moisture away, studying my fingers as they, too, begin to tingle.

Bastien stands behind me and spins me around, pressing me against his chest and enveloping me in subtle spices and the outdoors. Immediately, I am rocked by a surge of warmth that bathes me in an undeniable sense of protection. Given the circumstances, I don't protest because his safety is the only constant I have right now. I can't see him, but I feel his raging freight train heartbeat roar to life beneath my cheek. Then his breath is by my ear.

"Remember you are half vampire, and you aren't on suppressants anymore. I don't know how big a problem the rain will be, but don't you worry; I'll keep you safe."

All I can do is nod, the pinpricks against the back of my neck shifting into deeper burns. He lifts my collar higher, takes a step off the porch, and launches us into the heart of the storm.

26
ZERO GRAVITY

Bastien

POWER LIKE MINE IS a tricky, tricky thing.

There was a time when I manipulated energy without thinking. It was like breathing; it just happened. The Mothers made me that way.

And decades ago, when the vampire assassins swept through our ranks, I almost fell with my brothers and sisters. I released a flood from my core to try and save them, and I almost lost myself in the process. I failed, and the fallout nearly broke me.

I swore I would never open that part of me again but I cannot deny Octavia. She needs me, even if she doesn't know it yet.

She is pressed against me as I fight with the wind to get clear of the towering storm clouds. I don't want to push too fast with her in my arms. Her body already has been through enough hell. Shielding her from the rain takes concentration, and I can't move like I want to until I get her situated. Luckily, it only takes a minute or two to break into the calmer, open air.

I tighten my hold on her and let my energy encase us both. Her head falls back as her muscles relax. I slide my hand up the back of her neck to cradle it in my hand, and just before I am ready to launch, she opens her eyes.

In this moment, all I see is trust. It is the first time I have seen Octavia as she really is, not wound up and frantic, not angry and confused. There is magic inside of her that I don't recognize, but it is familiar in a way I can't explain. Before she closes her eyes again, I swear I see her smile.

And this is where it all changes.

27

BRAVE NEW WORLD

Octavia

"Hey, *cher*. We're here."

Bastien's voice is quiet; it is silky-soft and gentle in my ear. I open my eyes and, after I pull away from him, I see we are in a forest lit with eerie light. The skin on my face stings, and my eyes are blurry from keeping them closed for so long, making the scene in front of me even more ethereal. Add in the warm buzz of magical flight slowly draining from my body, and I'd almost believe I was dreaming.

"We're in the Wilds," he says quietly, tucking strands of my hair behind my ears. "This is the best place for you right now. They can help you make sense of what's going on, and they can keep ol' Andra in check. Human witches don't got not nothing on the fae, that's for sure."

Bastien smiles and chuckles. He looks different again, gentler. More like the man I've come to know.

"What did Andra and the other Mothers want with me that was so bad?"

Bastien begins to answer me, but out of the corner of my eye, I see the air wavering just beyond an arched footbridge. Then, as if she were stepping out of a vertical pool of water, Leelee emerges, followed by two other fae. They cross the bridge and pass an old jeep parked in a makeshift gravel parking area. I recognize one of them from the Mothers' house, but the other, a man, is unfamiliar.

"Thank you, Bastien," Leelee says as she takes my arm. "I'm sorry I couldn't bring you with me through Barataria, but a time tunnel is quite a bit different from the prism we have cast here."

There's a regal air about her here — less of a strange little being and more like a mystical wise woman. She tilts her head in Bastien's direction.

"She will be safe here until things become clearer."

Bastien doesn't say anything. His eyes are fixed on me.

"Bastien," Leelee leans around me, the dissipating energy between Bastien and I making my knees shake. Finally, he relinquishes his stare and blinks, straightening his already stiff spine.

"What do you want me to tell Andra? She'll be at my place already, if I know her like I do."

"Nothing." Leelee shakes her head. "If you and Octavia are gone, she'll know what's happened. Humans aren't the ones who hold Kretarie loyalty; we do."

I don't even know what's happening. A week ago, I was taking a clandestine trip to the grocery store to feed my Oreo addiction, and now I am standing beside a winged man outside some kind of portal to a fae settlement in what I assume is still Louisiana. It could be Narnia, for all I know. Nothing would surprise me anymore.

"Leelee," I pull my arm from hers and step away, wrapping my arms around my waist. "I don't want to be here. I want to find Seth. The plan was to go get Seth back." Silence descends around us. "Right?" I look to Bastien.

"Ah, *cher*..." he starts as he rubs the back of his neck. His eyes flare as he steps back, the trees erupting in a cacophony of bird calls as Auralie drops to the ground beside us. I move back to Bastien's side instinctively, half hiding behind his wing.

"Damn, y'all," she starts, a little out of breath. "You got a hornet's nest swarming back home. Leelee, Andra is heading this way."

Leelee's brow furrows.

"She knows she can't just show up here."

"Does she?" Auralie raises her eyebrows. "She's sure as shit gonna try, especially since a couple of Dormande goons started snooping around y'all's house in the middle of the night."

I feel it when Bastien bristles.

"Nah," he snarls, glaring at Leelee. "This is getting too close for comfort."

He reaches around my waist and pulls me close. "It's been a long time since we've tangled with any of the families. We can't risk being unprepared again. Remember, Auralie and I are all you have right now—"

"You have her." The fae woman I recognize lifts her chin in my direction.

My eyebrows shoot up. "*Me?* What am I supposed to do?"

"She can't do anything to help right now," Leelee chides. "She doesn't even know what power she has."

"Not yet," the man adds, his eyes harsh and probing in the low light.

"Power?"

What are they talking about?

A gust of wind sends a shower of leaves fluttering down, followed by a rumble of thunder. Leelee scans the sky, then looks back at me.

"You're right. She doesn't." She tilts her head in my direction then addresses the man behind her. "But we can help her from the safety of the enclave."

This is too much.

Hear them out, cher.

I glance up at Bastien as he gives a slight nod.

"No!" I pull free from Bastien's grasp. "You can't force me to stay here. None of you can tell me what to do. You've just been using all your crazy witchy magic stuff to scare me into staying, but I'm done with this! If Seth's family is coming for me, then he is in even more danger. We have to go. He needs help!"

Thunder rumbles in the distance, and we all look at the sky, but it's still clear here. Stars are twinkling between the boughs of tall trees. I put my hands on my hips and turn a slow circle to take a good look around, then my arms fall to my sides. I honestly don't know who I'm kidding. Do I plan on walking? I don't even know where I am.

"Octavia," Leelee says in a low, soothing voice as she approaches me. "I know you are worried about him. Perhaps if you tell us more, why he's different and needs to be rescued, we can help."

"He's not like them! He can't hurt me, but they don't... they don't know that." My eyes well up as tears threaten to fall, which makes me even angrier. "But they have him now, and they'll hurt him if they figure it out. They would do anything to be able to drink all types of blood. *Anything.* They'll... they'll..." I can't finish the sentence, refusing to think of what they'll do. Bastien moves closer.

"Octavia, listen to me." Leelee glides in front of me, intercepting Bastien as she grasps my hands and holds them up to her heart. "You are a precious thing. One-of-a-kind."

"So is he!" Her face blurs, my cheeks burning.

"So it seems." She squeezes my hands. "And while his people may view him as a resource to exploit, we see you as a treasure. If you let us help you unlock what you can do, you can lead the charge to save him."

"What if it's too late?" My voice comes out in a fragile whisper. I feel like I am being strangled by my fear while choking on my anger. *I can't breathe.* No one speaks. The wind settles into a constant breeze as muted flashes dance along the edge of what horizon we can see through the trees.

"What if it isn't?" Auralie breaks the silence. "Bastien and I can gather more information. Maybe we can confirm where your boyfriend is being held."

"I'll find him." Bastien's words are quiet. His eyes find the bracelet on my wrist. "That his?"

I lift my hand. The wolf's head bracelet dangles and shines in the pale light. *But I already know where he is. We're running out of time; I can feel it.*

"I can get a lock on his energy, maybe get some kind of idea of his condition, if I have something of his in my hands."

The irony of Bastien's words are not lost on me, but I unclasp the chain and hand it over. As Bastien's hand closes around it, he looks away.

"Come with us, Octavia. Let me help you unravel your own story before you decide to do something rash." Leelee releases my hands and walks toward the shimmering air.

There's a war raging inside me. I want to rush out of this place and find Seth. My legs ache to run until I collapse, but I can't head off all alone, no matter how delusional I am about my ability to hold my own. I know nothing about myself, nothing about what I am and what I can do. I hate it, but Leelee is right.

"I'll give you a day," I murmur, waiting for the fae before to agree before I turn to Bastien, who cannot hide his relief. "Can you hear me from far away? You know," I tap my temple, "in here?"

"Never tried, but don't you worry, *cher*." He reaches out and grasps the back of my neck, leaning forward to place the softest kiss against my forehead. It's surprisingly platonic. "I'll be right here this time tomorrow." He gently squeezes before backing up a few steps and gesturing to Auralie.

I have never actually *watched* a Kretarie take flight. I've only experienced it, so I am dumbstruck as I watch Bastien's wings open and his body tense, muscles tightening and bunching hypnotically before he pushes off the ground. Auralie follows and as they gain altitude, they leave a faint trail of wavering light behind them. In seconds, they are meteoric, just a streak of light fading into the starlit night.

"Come, Octavia." Leelee gestures to me. "Let us see what we can learn."

Reluctantly, I take her hand and take one last look at the night sky before I close my eyes and step through the wavering air.

28

THE STORY OF MY LIFE

Octavia

"OCTAVIA?"

The tiniest voice, as if it were a gentle breeze, sounds from beside me. I open my eyes, not prepared for what is in front of me.

We are standing in the same clearing we just left, yet past the edge of the clearing there are low, stone buildings integrated with the surrounding trees. More ghostly lights hang and float in and around the moss-strewn tree branches. Bunches of brightly colored azaleas are scattered around, their vibrant petals punching through the nighttime shadows.

"This is Briarwood," Leelee says, pride in her voice. "It is one of our hidden enclaves."

Turning slowly on my heels, my mind whirls as I try to take it all in. "Do all the fae live in places like this? I thought you were farmers and ranchers. It doesn't look big enough for that."

She smiles.

"Enclaves are small. It is where we practice our magic and meet when we need to ensure our privacy. No one can enter without an accompanying fae."

I cannot take my eyes off the ornate details surrounding me. Once, as a child, I was taken for a drive that wound through a fae settlement, but it looked no different from the town I resided in. This is most certainly not the same.

Leelee stops next to me, looking around her sanctuary. "So many questions, yes?"

"That's an understatement," I murmur.

"Let's sit and talk. I want to make the most of the time you have allowed me."

She leads me into the shadowy recesses until we reach a dwelling tucked between two exceptionally large trees. It looks as if the back of the structure has been built out from one of the tree trunks, and the other one arches out of the ground near the doorway like a sentinel.

She opens the door, a small smile on her lips, and we duck inside.

The space is dimly lit, but what light that is present is warm, not foreboding. A small table with two chairs is situated by a natural rock hearth, where a low fire crackles. It looks like a scene from a fantasy cottage. I glance up, my heart strangely calm. All it needs is a talking cat or an owl perched in the rafters.

"Sit with me, Octavia." Leelee gestures to the other chair. I collapse into my seat, still amazed at the way she has changed. At the Mother's house, she gave the appearance of a quirky old lady who moved to the beat of her own drum, but when she stepped out of the portal, her presence was so much more. Even the pitch of her voice has lowered.

Who is this woman?

"You are exceptional, you know." She sits back and lets her fingers toy with tiny ridges in the rough-hewn table.

"I gathered as much." I look away, letting my gaze fall on the gentle flames dancing in the fireplace. Where do I begin?

"How did this happen?" I clear my throat and shift my gaze back to Leelee. "How did *I* happen?"

She hums, seemingly pleased with my question.

"After you left us yesterday, we discussed this very thing. None of us," she gestures to herself, indicating the fae, "knew of anyone who had gone against the mandate."

"The mandate?"

She smiles apologetically.

"We generally frown on inter-species involvement. It isn't natural."

Fantastic. I'm a half-breed, and now I can add 'unnatural' to the list. I was different enough as an uncollected

A-negative human, but the label of 'unnatural half-breed' stings more than I imagined it would, and I shift in the chair.

"I had heard of a few fae outliers that wanted to try to open channels between humans and fae, but never between us and vampires." She can't disguise the distaste creeping into her tone, and I am officially offended.

I lean forward, placing my elbows on the table.

"I don't care how anyone feels about it. I am here. I exist. Now what?" I see I have struck a chord with her by the way her brow furrows.

"This is new territory, Octavia. I know nothing about your potential or the dangers you face." She shifts in her chair and leans forward, too. "This is why I wanted you here. Humans, even witches, have no stake in this now. It is only the fae or vampires that can make sense of what you are and of what you face. Vampires are enemy number one, so naturally, the fae are your best ally right now."

"Then we should get busy because this time tomorrow, I'm out the door." I lean forward even more to match her energy. "And I can leave with good, helpful information, or I can go out there blind. It doesn't matter to me."

She purses her lips but attempts to smile. I bare my teeth right back. I can see right through her. No one thinks I should go after Seth.

Fine. I don't need them to.

"There have always been fae who kept to themselves. Fae who didn't follow all our ways. We think your father was one of them."

My anger slips. "Why not my mother?"

"Fae births are few and far between. Though our males are virulent, our society has no stipulations on relationships. There are a great many fae women who partner together and have no interest in bearing a child. Additionally, the fae anatomy is very particular, and carrying a child any larger than one of our own would most likely risk the mother's survival."

I don't know anything about fae anatomy, so I have to trust that she makes a fair point.

"Do you have any idea who my father is?"

She shakes her head.

"With time, we could most likely find that out, but not tonight. There are more important things we must discuss." She turns in her chair and pulls a tablet from a shelf behind her. The light illuminates her face when she turns it on.

"Tonight, we must identify what power will manifest when your suppression fully wears off, if it hasn't already. We don't really know what has been given to you, though we can speculate."

"I felt the rain when we left Bastien's, so I think it's worn off." I sit back and hold my hands up to see them in the light. They are totally unharmed, but the memory of the sting is still there. "Am I the only fae-vampire?"

The words sound ridiculous. I feel stupid even saying it.

"As far as we know."

"Besides the obvious *mandate* issues, why would anyone work so hard to hide me?"

She sucks in a slow breath through her nose. It's obvious she is searching for the right words.

"Someone knew how special you were at your birth, and that someone knew you would be coveted. Rightly so."

Leelee mumbles and sets the tablet down and crosses her arms on the table, thinking as she reads through the text. Finally, she sits back.

"Aside from the anatomical constraints I told you about, there are other barriers to interbreeding between species. For example, almost all fae flow with magic, unlike our human cousins. It is the reason you are so unlikely. In our experience, only humans with the ability to touch magic, like a witch, could populate with the fae. Conversely, a rare fae that is numb to magic could produce a half-human child. Even then, offspring are highly unlikely."

"But not impossible, right?" I sit up straighter.

She shakes her head, her grey and silver curls catching the firelight.

"Nothing is ever impossible," she whispers. "Look at you."

We sit quietly for a few minutes. Leelee is swiping through the tablet screen, reading text I can't make out. I'm starting to learn how to roll with informational blindsides, but there are only so many bombshells one person can take.

A thought occurs to me.

"So, you say nothing is impossible, right?" I push away from the table and stand. "And as far as you know, both parents need to have magic, or they both must be completely devoid of it in order to have a child."

Leelee confirms with a single, slow nod. She's becomes distracted by what she's reading on the tablet.

"And you are positive I have vampire blood?"

Leelee appears to be only half-listening to me.

"Oh, yes," she murmurs as she taps and swipes the screen, her brow furrowed in concentration.

Biting my lip, I try to make all the pieces of my life fit together.

"That means there are vampires who possess magic. That's why I'm here, right? But are vampires supposed to have it? Magic?"

"They are not," she starts. "But neither are humans. However, fae ancestry is connected to human bloodlines; this is how human magic users are born. Far-flung and rare genetic throwbacks."

"That doesn't explain my mother. My *vampire* mother has to possess magic."

"She most certainly had to. Or your father was powerless."

I flinch at Leelee's use of the past tense.

She reaches out with one hand and whispers, her tone soft, "Do you feel it yet?"

I don't answer. My confused expression says it all.

"Your power. Have you felt it yet?"

"I don't know what you mean."

She grunts in the back of her throat. "Your boyfriend took you to the scientist often, yes?"

I frown, still not following.

"I think he took you because vampires want to learn about our power. They want to tap into it, even if they don't have the ancestry. The war between our kinds has raged for a thousand years, and they are eager to keep the upper hand. Your boyfriend may not have known, but I believe that scientist was studying you — experimenting on you. Using you to understand us."

"But why would vampires sense me when I bleed? If I'm not A neg, what are they smelling?"

Leelee leans back, her face more tired than I'd ever seen it. "They are scenting a vampire with fae power — something that shouldn't exist. It's their nature to attack the unknown."

"Why didn't Seth? It made sense when we thought I was A negative."

"Now that is a mystery, isn't it?"

29
BEHIND THE MASK

Seth

"Yes, Mr. Dormande." Illion growls before his cell phone ricochets off the wall.

A conceited satisfaction blooms within me.

"Let me guess. Going back on his word?"

As horrible as I feel, I can't help but laugh as I try to lift my head as far as the restraints of the exam table will allow. Illion is pacing across the room like an irritated cat. He stops, curses to himself, then disappears through the door.

"Whatever he's promised, you know he won't deliver!" I let my head drop back onto the table and try to stifle a groan.

Sounds of metal and glass clacking come from the next room, heavy footsteps growing louder just before Illion returns. I tremble in anticipation of what is coming, but my anger tempers the fear. He enters the room with his brow furrowed, his face etched in a deep scowl. His hands are gripping the tray so hard his knuckles are as white as the bone beneath his skin.

"What did he tell you he'd give you, Illion?" I growl.

He turns his back and ignores the question.

"Did he claim he'd give you a lab? Free rein? Unlimited resources?" Still, the old vampire keeps his back to me. "It's all a lie," I whisper.

"Do you truly think I don't know that?" Illion snarls as he whirls around to face me.

My eyes narrow. He's so close to exposing a chink in his armor. *Torture be damned.* If I keep pressing, I might just find out what it is, but if I push too hard, he will lock me out and things will only get worse. I've known him all my life, so I just have to think about what I know makes him tick.

"It stings, doesn't it?" My voice is a whisper now. "Being let down when all you want is a little recognition."

"You think you are being clever?" Illion shakes his head and smirks. "How adorable."

I know I'm not going to get any further with him, so I relax my muscles and sag back on the table to appear like I am growing too weak to argue. He needs to think I'm weak, even though I feel stronger than I have since he brought me here.

He can't know.

The only indication that I'm conscious is my chest's slow rise and fall. Out of slitted eyes, I watch Illion study a vial of blood in his hand before he returns his attention to the tray and the various beakers and tubes scattered across it. As soon as his back is to the exam table, I snap my eyes open and flex against the leather cuffs securing me to the table.

"This ruse is so sad, Seth. You can't get out of the restraints." Illion chuckles, his back still turned. "You know that. Enough with the theatrics."

I'm not thinking clearly. How many times have I watched Tavi do the same? I can't help my grimace when I sigh, my body slack against the warmed stainless steel.

"Just let me go, Illion. Nothing will come from this for you, at least nothing good where my father is concerned."

"That's where you're wrong, my boy. Your father has no part to play in my plans. However, *you* do." He pulls up the rolling stool to sit near my head, lazily tipping the sealed vial over my face. "Together, you and I will redefine the way the world views our kind. Do you think our inability to drink all blood makes us strong?" He scoffs, the glass cracking beneath his rage. "It does not. We, as a species, can only flourish as much as A negative humans do. *Don't you see?* We are the dependent species. I am destined to end that, and you? You are the key to our salvation."

"I will never help you, *you spineless fuck.* I thought my father was depraved, but you give that word a whole new meaning." I can't spit the insult with as much hate as I feel, my tongue heavy as I eye the glittering red in Illion's palm.

I fix my eyes on the ceiling, the blood thrumming in my ears. I can't believe this is happening. Never in a million years did I think Illion was playing me. He was a central figure in my life.

An uncle.

A trusted ally.

A friend.

And I let him put his hands on Octavia. The thought wrings a groan from my throat.

"You are right about one thing, Seth. Your father will never understand my superior wisdom. He will try to contain me. Control me. So, no, I don't want anything from your father. Truth be told, I'd rather not be *granted* anything, especially from him. He has no vision. No drive. His reign is stagnant. We deserve someone with purpose at the helm."

There it is.

The fool wants to usurp Arthur Dormande. That makes him crazier and more dangerous than I ever imagined.

"You want to take on the Directorate?"

He strokes my hair in the creepiest way.

"If only it were that simple. Just know I need to stay in your father's good graces for a while longer, no matter how much bowing to his idiocy it pains me." He pops the stopper off the vial. "Or you."

30

HEAVEN HELP ME

Bastien

As the Houston skyline comes into view, I cannot get the image of Octavia, soaking wet and coming apart at the seams on top of the Dormande skyscraper, out of my mind. It was like picking up a drowning kitten, full of spit and fury wrapped in frailty and desperation.

'I'm not sure what we'll be able to find. Did you get it?'

I glance at the bracelet in my hand, then back to Auralie as we gain altitude, my lips thinning. The air is quiet here, but it won't be for long.

'I did.'

'Can you attune to it? Or do you want me to try?'

Do I want to attune to an object that belongs to Octavia's boyfriend? I can't stop my frown from forming at the sight of the onyx snarling wolf's head. I don't want to get that close. But I need Octavia to see he's lost to her, that her blind faith in him still being the same person is wasted. It will hurt her, but it's necessary if I am to protect her like I am supposed to.

'I'll do it.'

Leaving Octavia at Briarwood was so much harder than it should have been. She acts tough, like she could waltz into a vampire stronghold, make her demands, and get what she wants. Maybe she can one day, but not right now. She's a walking time bomb, an unimaginable mass of twisted magic finding its way out of the twenty-year cage it has been held in.

I close my fingers around the bracelet and let my magic do its work. Seth Dormande's energy trickles into my grasp, and its signature surprises me. My heart sinks. He is different from the others, just as she described.

I adjust my grip on the bracelet, looking to find some negative trace of energy, but love radiates strongly, and it is attached to Octavia, though I pick up some notes of his mother. Anger resonates, but it's hard to discern all the different targets. But it is protectiveness that dominates everything I am sensing. I flinch. He would do anything for her, to the point of self-destruction.

Not my finest moment, but I had hoped to discover a more nefarious intention, and I don't find it. I loosen my grip on the wolf's head and let the thick chain dangle from my hand as I eye the thick pine forest below. Dropping it would be so easy, but that's not my way. I made a promise, and I intend to keep it no matter how I feel about it.

My focus pulls me northwest.

'We go this way now.'

I bank and Auralie trails behind, my emotions escaping their tight leash. The ground below us darkens as we follow the interstate highway into the hills of the piney woods. Here and there, small towns cluster and throw a spot of light onto the low-hanging clouds.

Wind gusts buffet my wings, prompting me to take a quick look back at the incoming hurricane. At this altitude, the storm and I are eye-to-eye with nothing blocking my view. It has grown, cloud tops forming an anvil that glows blue and orange with each lightning burst. The humid air skims across my skin. The brewing storm reflects the turmoil within me.

From the first moment I touched Octavia, something awakened. She is magic and science, electricity and earth, and the more I am near her, the more I cannot be without her.

'Yeah, yeah — look at the pretty colors. Mon Dieu, Bas! Focus!'

Auralie circles me, and her side-eye is visible, even in the dark. She's right. This ends faster if we can get a lock on Seth's whereabouts. My magic settles on the single line of lights that branches off from the interstate. I hesitate to follow them into the dark expanse of the pine forest.

'C'mon now, do what you do.'

Auralie gestures to the bracelet in my hand.

I could lie.

I could follow the energy, claim it faded, and tell her Seth is lost. My heart clenches, my breath catching. The fallout would be catastrophic. And that would make me a thief and a liar.

Against my instincts, I home in on the tug I feel coming off the bracelet. We aren't close yet, but the hum is building. I weave through the air to gauge a more accurate location, all the while giving me more time to make peace with Seth being alive. I can't make out anything more than his location, but the closer we get, the more I will be able to sense.

I promised to find him, so that's what I will do. If his energy has shifted, if he's giving off one ounce of danger, there won't be a Seth for her to find. But if he hasn't changed when she finds him, I don't know if I trust Octavia to know what's best for her, so come hell or high water, I'll be right there to pick her up when her world falls apart.

31

TOMORROW WAITS

Octavia

"I NEED TO GET out of here, Leelee."

She looks up from the table. I try to keep from sounding frustrated, but I can't help it. I am.

We've talked for hours, and I still don't know more than I did when we started, except that my parents might have had power... or they might not have? I rub my forehead, desperate for *something* to click into place. Leelee has tested me, scrutinized me, and studied me but given no indication she learned anything new.

I am exhausted, but the nagging anxiety of inaction is stealthily marching into my consciousness. I'm jittery and I can't sit still, which is why I've found myself across the room from her, alternating between an overstuffed chair and a cushioned window seat. For hours, there has been no mention of Seth, and I am getting the impression she is keeping me distracted to avoid my demand.

There's no telling what time it is, and there is no clock to check, even though I keep glancing around as if I will find one. Leelee explained that where we are is a one-dimensional fold off of our own reality, so daytime, nighttime, and other environmental things like seasons have no effect here. It is in a "perfect permanent state", whatever that means.

"How can I persuade you to stay?" She stands, gathering the books strewn across the table before crossing the room to where I sit. "I am so close to understanding where to begin unlocking your power."

"We have the rest of my life to figure that out, but Seth may not have the rest of the day."

She frowns with a shake of her head.

"Your suppression is nearly gone. You have no idea what traits you have inherited!" She lifts the books as if she's presenting evidence. "Everything I have read so far tells me you are a combination that *has* to be trained, or you must be suppressed otherwise you'll be dangerous to yourself."

"So, suppress me!" I don't mean to raise my voice, but I cannot continue negotiating with her. "Suppress me, and after I find Seth, you can do whatever you want."

"It's not th-"

"Not that easy? Of course it isn't. I'm not dumb enough to think that." I'm pacing now.

She sets the books down and grabs my arm when I pass her. Her grip is stronger than I expected.

"You know nothing about *any* of this!"

That's the loudest I have ever heard her speak, and I fear she may actually be angry with me. Her brow is furrowed; her grip is painfully tight. She drags me to the door, pulling us both outside.

"How will you leave the enclave? How will you return? Do you even know where you are? Are you planning on walking?" Her hand relaxes its hold, but she's clenching her teeth and pulling in a long breath through her nose before she drops my arm. She sighs heavily. To say I am taken aback is an understatement, and I guess my face says it all because she wrings her hands together and reverts to the diminutive, soft spoken woman I first met.

"I'm sorry, Octavia. You did not ask for this."

She's damn right I didn't. Leelee looks dejected, and though I have a fleeting pang of sympathy, it passes. Seth is the most important thing right now.

"I will let you go, but I have to be certain you understand the risk."

My eyebrows raise at her sudden willingness to acquiesce.

What's the catch?

"There's no trick to the portal. Once you have been allowed to pass through, it will open for you whenever you want it to. You only *need* it to open in here." She taps her chest, just above her heart. "You can take the jeep that's parked across the bridge. There's a map in the glove box."

My eyes narrow, and I hesitate to agree, but the chance to leave is too exciting to walk away from. While I am running all the possible gotcha scenarios in my head, she scurries back into the cottage and returns with a woven string backpack.

"There's a rain poncho in here. You mentioned the rain affecting you earlier, and with each hour that passes, your traits continue to bloom. It's not much, but it will help." She hands me the pack and presses a set of keys into my hand, her hand lingering before she releases her grip. "Just promise to think before you act and do not put yourself in a position to be taken by the Dormandes. We got you out once, but even Bastien would be hard-pressed to get you back a second time."

What an odd thing to say. I get it — he's a badass, but he's not the only one. Add that to my growing list of 'What the hell did that mean?'

Silence hangs thick between us, and I avoid eye contact, watching my feet as we make our way to the portal. When I look up, it is right in front of me, the rippling air so strange it locks my feet in place. I reach out to touch it, but it feels like nothing; it is just the air in front of me.

"Remember, you have to manifest need to come back through."

"Both ways?" I look at Leelee out of the corner of my eye.

She closes her eyes and nods. "I don't think manifesting need to leave will be a problem. That will make your first time passing through easier."

She's so right. I was ready to leave before I even got here. I tuck the keys into my pocket and give her one last look before I lock in on my need to leave, my need to get to Seth, and step through.

32

TASTE

Seth

MY LUNGS STRUGGLE AGAINST my desperate need for air, and it's all I can do to breathe. Illion nearly bled me dry before dumping me back in my cell. I can't tell how much time has passed, but it can't have been too long. My body would have recovered given enough time, but I don't feel the familiar healing that should be happening, and that scares the shit out of me.

My hands splay wide on the cold concrete floor, and there's an ache in my back I can't reach. He's done something to me, but what? I close my eyes; my sensitive hearing picks up a rhythmic clicking emanating from behind. I try to slide my arm behind me so I can feel for the tight, painful spot on my back, but I can't even get my hand off the floor. I don't have enough strength.

I don't know how long I can keep this up. The easy way out is tempting, if I could accomplish it, but as a vampire I can't. I am forced to stay strapped in on this ride Illion has put me on. I grit my teeth against the swell of desperation. I'm trapped.

To stop from losing myself completely, I let my thoughts drift to Octavia — my Tavi. My breath comes a little easier as I try to remember her scent and the feel of her skin. But memory backfires, and my peace crumbles as I recall the last time I touched her. She was scared and in pain from whatever Illion had been doing to her these last three years. And now she is lost to me, either in the hands of my father or the Kretarie.

And it is my fucking fault.

Noises I don't dare try to identify sound from beyond my cell. I delivered her to Illion on a silver platter over and over again, and it makes me sick. She trusted me, and I failed her. Now she is alone and suffering, and it's because of me. It's better that she's gone. She has a chance, at least.

Scenes from our last three years play out behind my closed eyes.

The first time I took her to Illion.

The first time I kissed her.

The night I stole her out from under my father and my brother.

I will never forget the look in her eyes when she realized I wasn't there to hurt her. One moment, she was terrified, thinking her life was over; the next, when she realized I was there to save her, I could have reached out and touched the hope and relief pouring off of her. She was seared into my soul from that moment.

I can't give up. We belong together, and she's out there. Kretarie or not, I have to hang on and find her. She'd do the same for me.

As I find the will to fight whatever Illion has in store for me, the door to my cell swings open and the monster himself enters with a blood-filled syringe. Just the sight of it makes my mouth water.

Fuck! Why aren't I healing?

"I bet you are famished," Illion drawls as he drops to a knee beside me. Oh, how I wish I could slap the fake sympathy off his face. I wouldn't hesitate if I could actually move, but I'm stuck on the floor, an impossible, anemic weight holding me down. His hand slips beneath my torso, groping for the line he inserted into my body.

"Now, this will only give you a little burst of energy." Illion produces the end of the line and attaches the syringe. "You'll bleed it out rather quickly because I have the pump rate set high. So," he pats my head like a puppy, "make hay while the proverbial sun shines!"

He depresses the plunger then stands, gesturing at the open door. My pulse quickens as the dose of blood spreads through my body. All of my senses roar to life when my body reacts.

A familiar scent laces the air, and a growl escapes my throat as Cain, my monster of a brother, the evil to my good, steps inside with a wicked grin on his face. He is exactly the same as the last time I saw him. Same stupid suit, same ridiculous jewelry; he is *always* the same egotistical asshat I wish I could forget.

"Hey, little brother," he purrs as a slow smile spreads across his face. He looks genuinely thrilled to see me in pain. "Guess you got yourself in over your head, hmm?"

"Still clinging to our birth order?" I seethe, my voice cracking from dehydration. I hate that I sound so pathetic. "Typical."

Cain yanks on a chain, and a human draped in a short hospital gown stumbles in behind him, hands chained together in front.

"I know you hate it when I'm right, but you need to eat. And this one," he pulls the young man close, leaning in to inhale his scent, "is very, *very* tasty."

Two fang marks dribble blood down the man's thigh, my mouth watering as my heart pounds. Cain likes to toy with his prey and finds amusement in biting them in places where the skin is more sensitive; he swears the adrenaline makes it taste better. I can't even look at him. He is the definition of perversion.

With another yank, Cain crouches down and attaches the chain to a metal ring on the floor. The man is right in front of me, his blood glistening within arm's reach. My fangs descend before I can stop them.

"You can't go very far from the pump line, but we've made sure your dinner is close enough to reach. And... he's just far enough to fuel your need to hunt," Illion says as he paces around the man.

Hunt? What the hell is he talking about?

"You look confused, Seth." Illion stands behind Cain, cocking his head to the side as he studies me. "If my intuition is correct, you should be feeling the urge to feed from our friend here any moment now. You are losing blood rapidly, so your instincts should be screaming to attack."

"I told you I won't give you what you want."

He's right, though. I cannot help the rough sound of my voice. My eyes flick to the man, then back to Illion and Cain.

"Oh, you can certainly try to abstain. Be my guest!" Illion chuckles as he saunters to the cell door, throwing a languid hand over his shoulder. "That's just more data for me to collect."

Cain's eyes glance back at the blood slowly dripping to the floor, his own fangs on display.

"You are finally going to reach your potential, brother." Cain crosses his arms and takes a slow backward step. "Then when the dust settles, and you are *fixed,* we can work together, the way father intended." He covers his heart with his hands and feigns empathy. "I have dreamed about this day for so long, and here it is."

They both disappear through the door, Cain's laugh echoing behind them, leaving me alone with the human chained in front of me. He shuffles backwards as far as the chain will allow, pulling it taut. The metallic aroma of his blood invades my senses, and as hard as I fight to contain my instincts, Illion is right. *I'm starving.*

My eyes lock onto the slowly growing puddle.

"Do you have to?" the man whispers. "I don't want to die."

My tongue traces the dry expanse of my lips. I could never differentiate between blood types like other vampires. Even A negative avoided detection because blood was blood. I relied on my mother to keep me supplied, and she never failed me. But now, the blood running down this man's leg sings.

And I need it.

"Please," he begs. His voice is quivering now. He knows what's going to happen.

Fight it!

I don't want this.

My father should have killed me when he had the chance.

Anything but this.

I cannot become what Octavia fears.

My mouth salivates, my muscles tighten and tense, and before I can stop myself, I am on him. He crumples to his knees when I attach myself to his neck. The flow of blood over my tongue burns, quickly fading to an irresistible tang I couldn't possibly satisfy. Warm blood like spiced honey pours down my throat. I have never tasted anything like it, and I don't want to stop.

"There," Illion's voice returns, the distortion through the speakers hardly noticeable. "A negative blood isn't so bad now, is it?"

33

ESCAPE

Seth

I DON'T REMEMBER THEM taking his body.

But they do, quickly replacing it with another.

And another.

And another.

Time runs together.

Maybe it's been days, or maybe it's been hours; I can't tell anymore. One by one, I am forced to feed, each victim with a different blood type, my hunger never fully satisfied. At some point, I stop being able to drink.

Even gorged to the brim, I'm still weak. I'm losing blood faster than I can replenish through my own healing. How Illion is syphoning me is not a mystery anymore. The tube inserted in my back is perfectly placed to where I cannot reach it, and it runs to the wall behind me. When I move, it retracts just enough to keep the slack unreachable, and my own chains keep me too far away from the wall.

It is a no-win situation. Faster clicks tell me he is upping the syphon rate, my body no longer able to hold itself up.

When my eyes open again, the metal ring on the floor is empty. Rage thunders through me, I am ravenous with a hunger that eats at me from deep in my belly. My only respite is to close my eyes and try to sleep through it. It's the only way I've survived Illion's special brand of hospitality until now, but before I can slip into oblivion, the door opens again.

"Wakey, wakey," Cain whispers. "Oh, baby brother, you look terrible." He chuckles and ruffles my hair, which only infuriates me more.

I keep my eyes closed.

What did I do to deserve this? I was didn't always hate Cain; it was quite the opposite, honestly. For most of my life, I tried to follow Cain's example and worked to please my father, even if I kept secrets from him. My mother made no bones about whom she favored, though.

But Cain? For most of my life, I stayed quietly in his shadow, avoiding the spotlight as much as I could. I was happy to let him have it all if my secret stayed safe, and even Cain kept it, despite this diabolical act he's playing at right now.

"This will go faster if you cooperate, Seth." He's crouched beside me. "I've seen the protocol. You are finally *doing* something for our family." His tone shifts, a dark edge creeping in. "Now, act like a Dormande."

"I was never good at lying, Cain," I mumble. "You, of all people, should know that." My eyes crack open enough to see the irritation etched on his face.

"Fine." Cain smirks and shakes his head as he injects something into my stomach port. He stands with his hands on his hips. "You don't have to want it. Hell, you don't even have to be willing. You're going to do it, so might as well give in. It'll be easier that way. Let's go!" he calls over his shoulder.

A pair of Directorate goons come through the door, each clutching a human in a hospital gown. One an older woman, so frail and weak she can hardly stand, and the other...

I'm going to be sick.

All the breath leaves my body at the same time the blood I've been given takes hold.

She looks just like Octavia.

"What fucking sick game is this, Cain?" I roar, bolting upright as the women are hooked to the metal ring. The older woman looks like she's in shock — no signs of fear, just wide eyes staring at me, dumbfounded. The other, younger one is terrified, her chest heaving with shallow, trembling breaths, but she looks ready to fight.

Everyone slips out the door as the three of us wearily eye one another. Before it closes, I hear Cain say, "Enjoy, brother."

"Just kill me already!" I scream, spit flying from my mouth as I slam the floor with my fists. Curling into a ball, I clutch my head, my nails painfully scoring my scalp.

I can't.

I won't.

I rock back and forth as whatever he injected into me ignites my whole body.

"I won't do it. I won't do it. I can't do it. *I can't!*"

But feral hunger stalks my sensibility, stealing the last shred of morality I have. I can smell them. Their fear. Their sweat. Their blood. I am intoxicated with the most addictive drug, and I can hear them breathing, one labored and the other nearly panting.

I can try to refuse and let them drain me. It'd be painless, a mercy compared to everything I've endured, but Illion won't allow it. No matter what, at least one human will die by my hands. My heart rate increases, and I feel my fangs extend.

It's coming, and I can't stop it. My head snaps in their direction. The Octavia lookalike pulls as far back as she can until the snap of the chain makes her lose her balance,, angry tears streaming down her face.

Please don't leave me here alone. You can't leave me here.

Octavia's voice echoes in my ears. She was crying when I left her at my mother's.

I left her.

No! She's not Octavia. Illion and Cain are messing with my head in this waking nightmare.

Fuck them.

Another sound, a low groan, drags my attention to the older woman. Her shock has worn off, and fear is taking hold. Her legs are shaking as she takes a few unsteady steps backwards.

There's nothing stopping me from taking her first.

With a snarl, I launch. She falls to the ground as I sink my fangs into her throat, a guttural sigh filling the air as her essence rolls over my tongue. Maybe she'll be enough. Maybe I won't have to take them both.

Resigned to my fate, my fingers leave bruises across her skin, but before I can swallow, I gag, blood dribbling down my chin.

This blood is wrong.

Tearing my teeth from her flesh, the woman screams and scrambles away from me. Without thinking, I stalk towards the younger woman, my hunger welcoming her fear.

No!

Stiltedly, I force myself to turn away. I need to feed off the older one. I have to. *I can't hurt Octavia.*

I crawl towards my first victim. This has to work. She's kicking at me, but it's too easy to grab her leg and yank. We both fall back as I bite again. I swallow, ignoring the screams behind me, before I retch it all back up.

"No, no, no!" I scream at the woman as her blood pours out of my mouth. Shock has set in and she is paralyzed by pain and fear. But I keep my attention fixed on her, my muscles threatening to snap bone as I stop myself from looking over my shoulder.

"What's wrong with you?" I beg while tears stream down my face. The need to feed rises, impatient with this setback.

Breathing heavily through my nose, I close my eyes and attempt to recover my control. But my body isn't having it. I teased it with fulfillment, gave in to my most basic desires, only to have it snatched away. A racing heartbeat laced with a delicious scent floods my senses.

Hunger engulfs me, and I raise up to my knees. Octavia's behind me, and I *need* to taste her. I *have* to. But when I turn and those eyes lock with mine, my heart withers and rage replaces the pain. These eyes are brown, not hazel. With a snarl, I attack, her screams fueling my need to drink her dry.

And I do.

34

HOW TO SAVE A LIFE

Octavia

'A HURRICANE WARNING IS in effect for portions of southwestern Louisiana and the Texas Gulf coast. Radar indicates the storm is slow-moving, but the latest models are predicting Hurricane Erika will likely make landfall somewhere between—'

I click the radio off. It's not telling me anything I don't already know. The wind picks up considerably as I pull onto the highway, gusts so strong that the semi in front of me sways dangerously over the line, fighting to remain steady. My knuckles go white against the wheel, my jaw tight in anticipation of the same force, but I don't feel it as I merge into the middle lane. Maybe it's dying down.

Dark clouds have been gathering on the horizon since I arrived in Louisiana. The Mothers warned there was a hurricane on the way, but I thought nothing of it until I slipped through the portal at Briarwood and looked up at the sky. Though I started my drive around noon, the storm darkens the day nearly into night. I have at least another four hours until I'm there, and this hurricane hasn't even made landfall.

The Jeep jerks as I careen through a puddle of water.

Leave it to me to attempt a rescue mission when a hurricane is about to hit.

The highway is mostly empty, save for a few semis and the occasional car slowly inching through the rain. The sky erupts with crackling tendrils of lightning like someone hit the world with a hammer and shattered it. The rain slams against the windshield while I crane my head to get a better look at the road.

Not good.

I sit straighter in my seat. Before, this kind of rain would have been an insurance policy, the streets almost safe for humans. Maybe I can still use this to my advantage. If it keeps up, the storm will make my approach to Illion's undetectable. My newfound sensitivity to water is a problem, though. With one hand, I tug the rain poncho out from the backpack and glance at its flimsy construction. I don't know how I'll get Seth out, but I'll worry about that when I get there.

The hours drag on, and my hands hurt from holding the steering wheel so tight. I'm skirting the edge of a panic attack between the storm and my nerves; I've had a long time to think. And now, adding fuel to my one-millionth impending freak-out, the gas gauge is dangerously close to the red line.

I check the bag Leelee gave me earlier, hoping for gas money or even a credit card, but no. Just a rain poncho and a couple of stale granola bars. Now, all I can do is keep going and hope for the best.

Hurricane or not, I will find him.

The engine hesitates, and my heart plummets. I tap the gas, hoping I imagined the sputter despite knowing I didn't. It lurches again, then dies as I lean hard on the wheel to guide the now useless shell to a stop on the gravel shoulder. The rain is coming down in sheets, lightning illuminating the night as bright as day. Desperation takes hold and tag teams with my escalating anxiety.

A crack of thunder rattles the car, and at that moment, utter hopelessness crashes into me like an ocean wave hitting me from behind.

Surely, Leelee knew I would need to get gas. I check all the gauges because this can't just be me running out of gas. Maybe she did it on purpose? If she did, this is some passive-aggressive bullshit way to keep me from finding Seth.

What am I doing?

I am in the middle of a hurricane in an old-ass Jeep - out of gas, out of time, and out of options. Even if Leelee's motivation wasn't duplicitous and she honestly let me leave her enclave to actually attempt this, the universe went all-in on stopping me. I don't see any way I can win.

As lightning flashes, I stare out at the road. Highway 21 cuts a narrow path through the tall trees — a direct line leading to the most likely place for me to find Seth and I can't move.

Rage erupts within me, and I scream a primal noise roaring to life from my deepest center. White-hot energy tears through my body, looking for release. My heartbeat pulses in time with the surging forces awakened inside me. A river of burning power breaks loose, and I channel the torrent of anger into my hands, hoping the wheel will break. Bright lights burst behind my eyes. I am a star collapsing in on itself, and I am going to explode.

Then the engine roars to life.

My breath catches.

Rain beats down on the windshield hard enough to almost drown out the purr of the motor. I'm stunned into silence, slowly opening my fingers as I release a shaking breath. The steering wheel vibrates against my palms, sending shivers up my arms - or maybe my arms send the vibrations into the wheel. I can't define where the sensation begins and ends because my body is boiling from the inside out.

In a daze, I press my foot on the gas, shocked when the car rolls over the gravel towards the road. When the tires meet the pavement, I drive like a bat out of hell. I'm not looking this gift horse in the mouth; I'm riding her Kentucky Derby-style until she drops.

Before time has a chance to register in my brain, the gravel and dirt track leadings to Illion's lab comes into view. The rain still pelts the pavement, thunder rolling through the sky while lightning flashes like fractures between heaven and hell. My body is hot but still shivering involuntarily as I climb out of the car.

Violent itching and burning overwhelms my exposed skin, the downpour relentless around me. I bite back a yelp as I fall back into the Jeep and yank out the poncho. With shaking hands, I pull the poncho over my head before slipping into the brush surrounding Illion's lab.

I have no plan.

Hell, I don't even know if Seth is here, but I creep forward regardless. Muted light glows from a window in the only above-ground room of Illion's hideout. The rain makes it hard to see, but eventually I find my way to the wood and aluminum paneled wall. Peering through the glass, I can see straight down a set of narrow stairs to Illion's study. Even the corner of the suede loveseat I curled up in so many times before is visible. My stomach turns.

The rain has intensified, the storm threatening to expose me as flashes illuminate the forest as brightly as the sun. My soaked feet and hands are on fire, but the pain ebbs and flows like I'm burning and healing in rapid succession. With a grunt, I push the pain into the back of my mind.

Seth is the only thing that matters.

Moving shadows catch my attention, and I press my forehead to the glass, cupping my eyes for a better look despite my potential exposure. I'm feeling reckless with this new wild power writhing inside of me.

A figure is crouched between the loveseat and the table that sits in front of it. Grumbling at the water on the glass, I use my poncho to wipe as much as I can away and brace my arm above my head as a shield to keep it clear.

My eyes burn. *It's Seth.*

He grabs the back of the loveseat and collapses onto his knees. Despite the rain and the fog on the glass, I see everything brighter and clearer than I should in this torrent, a byproduct of my newly discovered lineage.

His chest heaves. My heart races. Water drips from his face, so much so that it looks like he's just been outside in the deluge, but when he reaches up to wipe his eyes, soft lamplight illuminates his hand.

He's covered in blood.

Another lightning flash exposes my silhouette in the window against the basement wall, and Seth's head snaps up. His eyes are set deep in dark circles, and his fangs are out. My heart drops and steals my breath. I've never seen them fully exposed before.

Our eyes lock. His lip curls in a snarl, and he lunges, one of his bloody hands grabbing the arm of the loveseat. He contracts, his body curling in on itself.

My eyes widen. He's trying to hold himself back.

"Go," he mouths, eyes wide and wild. Then he turns his head away from me, toward a shadow moving behind him.

I don't know what to do.

"Seth," I choke on his name, his body blurring into a dark mass at the bottom of the stairs. Just as I raise my hand to the window, ready to test my strength, I'm flying backward into the air, the breath knocked from my lungs.

35
WRECKING BALL

Octavia

"You surely do know how to make things difficult, *cher*," a low voice rumbles in my ear.

Bastien? What is he doing here? I'm too shocked to even care that the wind whips the rain against my face, but finally I have to close my eyes against the pain lancing through them.

"Let me go!"

I thrash against his hold, while wings beat hard behind me. The steady pulse of Bastien's muscles and the warmth radiating off his chest soothes the acid sting of the pelting rain. He holds me tightly against him, his arms circling my waist and shoulders. I want to wriggle free, but then what? Freefall into the forest below?

Bastien's calming touch tries to fight against the anger and the intensity of my emotions, but this time he can't.

I know I'm being difficult, but I didn't come all this way to be retrieved like a dog that slipped its collar. A crash of thunder tears through the sky — the cracking and rumbling bolstering my resolve. Now I realize I'm feeding off the energy of the storm, so I embrace it.

Finally, Bastien can't manage my increasingly slippery form. He drops to the road below, and I stumble out of his grasp, whirling around to face him.

"What was that? Why are you here?"

He towers over me, his hands clenched in fists at his sides. The look in his eyes is unnerving - an intensity I've not yet seen.

"He'll kill you."

"Seth would *never* hurt me," I snarl, even though I'm not convinced that's true.

"That's not your boyfriend anymore. He'll rip into you without a second thought. He's already done it to others if the bodies are any indication."

Bodies?

"Behind the building. Most are fresh." Bastien sees my confusion and points back toward Illion's lab. "There must be seven or eight of them."

"It doesn't mean he did it!" My chest is heaving now, and I replay what I just saw through the window.

Seth.

Covered in blood.

No.

My eyes narrow as Bastien steps closer. The way he's looking at me keeps me from bolting.

"It wasn't him." My voice is quiet, shaking. I don't know who I am trying to convince — me or him. "He wouldn't hurt anybody."

Part of me still wants to turn back and do something stupid, but I cannot tear myself away.

"He's gone." He lifts one massive hand and cups my cheek. This time, I don't fight against his soothing efforts, siphoning his warmth as my skin recovers from the burning rain and my body calms. His eyes are fixed on mine, a hint of a smile curling his lips. "You've gotten your magic." His thumb brushes my temple. "I can feel it."

The power inside me hums louder.

"I have to go back," I whisper.

His smile dissolves.

"You can't help him, Octavia. He's not who he was anymore. He'll kill you, *cher*." He tightens his fingers in my hair and steps closer, leaning down. His other arm slides around my waist, his hand at the small of my back.

"But he'll have to go through me," Bastien vows just before our lips meet. The frenzy of the storm falls away as his warm energy envelops me, my newfound magic blossoming in response to his. Against all my better judgement, I'm losing myself.

"Wh-" I pull away, searching for words I cannot find. I'm confused and drowning in Bastien's embrace - an exquisite flood of fear and excitement I've never felt before thrumming through me. "How-"

A tree branch cracks behind us, and Bastien's head snaps up, his eyes immediately finding the source. He pulls me in tight, a low rumble in his chest.

"Oh, Octavia," a familiar voice calls, the manic excitement evident despite the storm.

My blood runs cold.

Cain.

My heart hammers in my chest, my hands gripping Bastien's shirt so tight it tears. Rain pelts my body, and I shiver as my exposed skin burns.

The rain.

How can he be out here? I try to spin around, but Bastien's faster. He pushes me behind him, stepping toward Cain. Squinting against the deluge, I lean around Bastien's wings to get a better look. Seth and Cain are identical twins, so telling them apart shouldn't be easy, but this one is covered head-to-toe in expensive-looking clothes, not blood, the hood of a rain slicker low over his face.

"That was fast." Cain points the pistol in his hand at Bastien - the snark in his voice solidifies his identity as his signature smirk warps his face. "I tried to tell my brother that you were only good for one thing, but," he takes a slow step forward, "he wouldn't listen."

"I'm taking her away from here, *fonchock*," Bastien snarls. "But I'll be back*, and I* will end this*.*"

A shot rings out from behind.

Bastien whirls around and is immediately over me, shielding both of us with his wings as we drop to a crouch. I look through a gap in Bastien's wall and see another figure. He's not covered up, though. The rain is visibly burning his skin as he points a shotgun toward the sky. Lightning flashes, glinting off a dragon pendant around his neck.

Seth.

I lean forward, preparing to lunge, but Bastien pulls in tight.

"No," he warns as he raises his head.

"Back away, Seth," Bastien shouts over a crack of thunder as the muscles in his arm contract against my waist. I watch Seth level the gun at us, his face expression-less.

"Seth!"

Seeing him like this is killing me, just like seeing me with Bastien must be devastating him, though you couldn't tell by looking at him.

"Oh, brother," Cain laughs from behind us. "Now we finally see eye-to-eye! You should have let me take her in when I had her."

I can't tell if Cain's coming closer over all the noise from the storm, but I don't dare take my eyes off Seth. A flurry of scenarios plays out in my head, and none of them are good. Seth takes a step in our direction.

"Take her." Seth is looking at Bastien and breathing hard, his hands raw from the rain. But he still shows no evidence of pain. "Get her away from me. Go!"

Bastien wraps his other arm around me, and I feel his muscles bunch as he prepares to take flight. The world spins - my heart breaking as rage builds in my belly and the wave of energy I felt before threatens to let loose again.

"Don't lose control," Bastien warns, his voice low in my ear.

But I don't know what to do with this new magic welling up inside of me. A wave of icy energy rises, and I want it to consume me. It is the most dangerous feeling I've ever known, but also the safest. Nothing can hurt me. I'm sure of it.

"Oh no, you don't, Kretarie." I hear Cain's footsteps gaining momentum now. "She's mine."

"Hold on," Bastien grunts as he pushes off the pavement. I'm oblivious to the ground falling away. Sound slows into a thrum while my bones ache and groan as time and space warp around me. I'm gripped by a glacial surge, expanding in a shockwave off my skin. I swear I hear the crack of a gunshot, but I can't see a thing because the lightning has found me.

Bastien jerks, his grip loosening as rain swirls around us.

Gravity takes hold, my stomach hollowing out as we fall.

Another shot fires.

We hit the ground, and Bastien is beside me, clutching his side.

"Bastien!" I scramble to my knees to see how bad he's hit, but as I do, I catch a glimpse of Cain nearby, less scared than I should be when I see he is down on one knee as blood pours from a gaping wound in his shoulder.

I don't even bother to look for Seth because something greater than rage rips itself free from my throat, splintering the surrounding air. My scream is visceral; my intent, deadly.

Everything goes dark.

36

READY FOR WAR

Genevive

"Where are you taking me?"

Both of my hands are bound in front of me, so it's easier for me to lean forward and study the man I stuck to. I lift my hands and pound on the center console of the Mercedes. My husband pretends to ignore me, but I see the muscles in his neck tighten with annoyance. I fall back and sigh.

"I get it, Arthur. You are in control."

He chuckles, setting my teeth on edge. He knows it agitates me more than anyone. If there is one thing that gets under my skin, it's being mocked. He smiles broadly, his chest puffing with pride.

The car shakes as it fights against the wind and the pooling water on the road. I can tell we are traveling north by the abundance of pine trees—it's hard to miss them swaying dangerously every time a flash of lightning illuminates the sky. This little adventure must be incredibly important for him to risk being out in a storm like this.

Finally, as we turn off the main highway, Arthur breaks his silence.

"You realize you are not as smart as you think, right?" The car slows. "You've been conceited in your self-assurance these past few years, believing I was clueless about your little escapades. If only you knew how much of your enterprise I control."

My breath catches, but I keep quiet because I know Arthur relishes the opportunity to tear me apart. He's very good at it.

"Nothing to say?" He glances in the rearview mirror. "No witty comeback? Darling, you disappoint me."

The car slows as Arthur guides it around a bend. The storm has intensified, and high winds are bending the treetops at dangerous angles. I keep my eyes fixed out the window, trying to maintain the appearance I am unaffected by everything.

An extraordinary burst of lightning illuminates the night, and Arthur slams on the brakes, flinging me forward against the seat in front of me. I push myself upright with my elbows and look out the front windshield.

"What the h-"

A man stands in the middle of the road, large wings spread open behind him, buffeted by the high winds. In his arms is a girl, and they both look at the forest's edge, where a dark, hooded figure has appeared. For a breath, nothing happens; the three appear stuck in time.

A tiny smile forms on my lips.

"Is that a Kretarie?" I whisper mostly to myself.

"A soon-to-be-dead one," Arthur growls as he makes for the door handle. Before he can lift the lever, a shot rings out, and we both jump. After the shock dissipates, the irony of our shared reaction is not lost on me.

The pair drop, the Kretarie's wings spread like a shield over them. In the silence, another figure, holding a shotgun, emerges from the forest, leveling it across the road.

I glance back at the hooded figure, who is closing the gap between himself and the Kretarie. Same height. Same walk. Shock slides over me like a bucket of cold water.

It all makes sense now. Two figures facing off against a girl and a Kretarie?

My boys.

Octavia and the Kretarie leap into the air, his powerful wings battling against the wind and rain. One twin runs for the Kretarie and fires a shot from a pistol. Arthur is just about to pull the hood over his head and rush outside when the crack of a shotgun stops him. My heart stops with him.

The Kretarie and the girl fall to the ground as I gasp — one of my boys cradles his shoulder while the Kretarie grips his leg. Octavia tumbles between them, but then she rises, and the sky lights up as five lightning bolts strike her. She screams - the air around her wavering and warping.

Then she's gone.

"What the..." I can't complete the sentence. In the space of a few seconds, my twin sons have appeared in the middle of a hurricane with firearms as a Kretarie, a creature no one has seen in decades, stood between them.

Arthur sprints from the car.

As he runs to our wounded son's side, the other pumps the shotgun and continues striding across the street. The lightning has slowed, making it difficult for me to see. If it weren't for our headlights, I wouldn't have seen another winged Kretarie drop from the sky, standing sentinel next to her injured compatriot.

She is a behemoth of a woman, and when she turns her back, the light reflects off her insect-like wings. I resist the urge to roll the window down for a better look. There's no time anyway. By the next flash of lightning, both Kretarie are gone.

I squirm and wriggle myself into the front passenger seat to get a better look at everything that is happening. Arthur left his door open, so I press against the opposite side of the car to avoid the errant splashes and drops from the storm. One twin stands before his father and brother, shotgun aimed squarely at one of them - I can't tell who is in the crosshairs, but now I know the twin with the shotgun must be Seth. Panic claws at my throat, my heart shattering in my chest. He's almost unrecognizable in the chaos — shirtless and blistering from the rain.

Arthur rises to stand over Cain. He reaches under the back of his waterproof jacket, and I know what comes next. Fighting to suppress my urge to dive into the rain, I cannot help calling out,

"Seth!"

Lightning flashes. Seth's hands, practically glowing red from his blisters, tighten on the shotgun.

Arthur lifts his pistol.

"Seth, run!" I scream.

My voice causes Arthur to hesitate, allowing my Seth to dart past his father, abandoning the shotgun on his way into the dense forest.

Arthur's face radiates anger once he realizes he missed his opportunity, and he wastes no time helping Cain to his feet and ushering him to the car. He stumbles, but Arthur catches him and shoves him in the back seat before climbing into the front and slamming his door.

"Hello Mother," Cain pants, his voice laced with a maniacal chuckle.

"Why?" I stare at my son who I just witnessed trying to kill his brother.

"Dad hasn't told you?" He scoffs, leaning his head back and closing his eyes. Letting himself sag to the side, he clutches his shoulder while taking shallow breaths. The bleeding has slowed, but what little of his face I can see shows he's waxy and pale. My lack of maternal instincts does not surprise me as I note that a few more inches to the left would have done the trick. He groans. "I'm healing, but I'm soaked, and it hurts like a son of a bitch. We need to get inside the lab."

Arthur already has the car in gear and is rolling toward the driveway ahead.

"We're here," Arthur growls. He looks over his shoulder. "Hang on, son."

I stare. None of this makes any sense. I start to say something but change my mind, snapping my mouth closed before the words can escape. As we pull up to the dilapidated shack, I notice Cain's black sports car already parked outside. Cain was here with Illion before we arrived, and I am certain that this rabbit hole has no end in sight. Arthur has outdone himself, and more importantly, me. The large garage door swings wide, allowing Arthur to pull inside and turn off the car.

My door opens from the outside, my jaw locking. It's Illion. His eyes glint as they scan over the three of us, the corners tightening ever so slightly. If I were further away, I would've missed it.

"You're quite the mess, Cain."

"If you hadn't let my cunt of a brother escape, I'd be in much better shape," he hisses through gritted teeth.

"Tsk, tsk...temper!" Illion chides as he nods to someone in the shadows to help Cain into the house. He looks at me. "I see you've brought the family, Cain. That wasn't our plan, was it?"

"Plans change. Are you ready to proceed?" Cain shrugs off Illion's man, still clutching his shoulder.

"Oh, so eager to hold the keys to the world, aren't you?" Illion hesitates as he spares Arthur a quick glance, then turns his attention to me. He pastes a saccharine smile on his gaunt, waxy face. "Hello, love."

My face sours at his far-too familiar term of endearment.

"Cain has been telling me about your latest endeavor," Arthur grumbles as he exits the car. "I thought it would be prudent to check your progress, considering that I was not informed about any of it."

Illion straightens, allowing Cain to fall back against the car.

"That is premature and *not what we discussed*." Illion's glare at Cain is pure venom.

Palpable tension builds between the three of them, giving me even more reason to stay right where I am. There is an undercurrent of derision between them, and I cannot miss an opportunity, especially if I am able to broker some sort of alliance between Illion and myself.

"You need his money, Illion. You'll thank me later," Cain shrugs and winces, grabbing his shoulder tighter.

"Illion, I always say you have to take risks, but you know better than to do things behind my back. As long as you benefit from my money, you are on *my* time. And now, you are under my direct supervision." As Arthur steps into the shadows, I watch Illion's face, his hatred positively radiant.

I knew they didn't see eye to eye, but I never realized it was this bad.

They detest one another. And now it seems that my son has driven the wedge between Arthur and Illion to the breaking point. Classic Cain.

Arthur wants something only Illion can produce, and I bet Illion would rather peel his skin off with a cheese grater that actually give Arthur what he desires.

A smile begins to form on my lips, but I stop it before anyone notices.

I can work with that.

37

OH MY, MY

Octavia

"TAVIA!"

I want to giggle but quickly stifle the sound. Hide-and-seek is my favorite game, and I'm very good at it. Actually, Daddy says I'm the best.

"Rikki Tikki Tavia," Daddy calls, using his silly pet name for me, "where are you?"

I strain to hear his footsteps, needing to decide when to run for home base. The sofa is two rooms away, and he's so much faster than me. I've been practicing, though - taking the lightest steps, imagining a cushion of air under my feet to keep them quiet.

I listen hard. He's going up the stairs.

My feet tingle as I dart out from behind the curtain. I feel so light this time. The round dining room table whizzes past me as I silently sprint. It's a straight line from my hiding spot to the living room.

I'm going to make i-

"Octavia!"

My mother catches my shoulders as I run across the hall.

"Mama!" I look toward the stairs, fumbling against her hands. She looks unhappy. Maybe she is sad because we are playing without her. "He'll hear you!"

Mama bends down and takes my face in her hands, looking me in the eye. She's frowning. "Stop running. You'll fall and hurt yourself." She straightens up when she hears my father, turning in his direction. "Mal, why do you encourage her?"

My mother brushes past my father as he reaches the bottom of the stairs, and he frowns at her back as she walks away. I know I shouldn't pout, but I can't help it.

"Good work, Tavia." He smiles as he ruffles the hair on the top of my head. "I didn't hear a thing. You are getting better and better at-"

"Octavia!"

I'm shivering.

No, that's not right. I'm shaking.

Someone is shaking me.

"How long has she been out?"

The voices sound far away. I'm trying to respond, straining to get my mouth to move, but nothing in my body is working.

"At least an hour."

I don't recognize the voices.

"What about Bas?"

"Auralie followed him when he left. I'm sure he's with her."

Okay, that's Leelee.

"Where is she hurt? She's bleeding."

"It's just a little scrape. A little road rash is all..."

I have no idea who besides Leelee is talking, but whatever has gotten hold of me is loosening its grip. Wincing, I pry my eyes open and gasp as the light sends shards of pain through my head. I curl protectively around myself, silently begging the pounding to stop.

"Dim the lights!" Leelee calls out, and the room darkens immediately.

The last few hours come crashing back into my mind.

The storm. The gunshots. Seth and Cain. And...

"Bastien!" I sit up. My mind is running wild and is tumbling around the last moments I remember with Seth and Cain. The room takes a turn. And just like that, I'm hyperventilating. Manon is beside me in an instant, propping me against her shoulder. Leelee scurries to my other side and places her hands on my arm.

"Where's Bastien? What happened to Seth?" I search her face. I know I'm frantic, but the last thing I recall was Bastien lying wounded between two armed vampires hell-bent on shooting someone. My eyes find the blood on the leg of my jeans. "Is that his?"

Pushing away from Manon, I sit up on my own, surprised to find I'm on the Briarwood cottage floor.

"Who brought me here?" I crawl onto my hands and knees, painfully folding my legs under me so I can stand. "How did I get here?"

Manon scrambles to my side again, and realizing my unsteadiness isn't going away, I let her support me with her arm. I drop my head and close my eyes, needing to stop the room from spinning. *In through my nose. Out through my mouth.* As soon as I feel like I can open them without throwing up, I look back at Leelee.

"Leelee, is that Bastien's blood?" I *need* to know.

She's about to answer me, but I hear a ruckus outside the front door before it swings open.

"I don't bleed, *cher.*"

Bastien limps into the room, supported by Auralie, but as soon as he sees me, he is pulling me from Manon's grip. My racing heartbeat slows as he slips one arm around my waist, his other looping beneath my knees, scooping me into his arms. I can tell he's in pain by his grimace and the subtle way he narrows his eyes.

"You're hurt," I protest, halfheartedly wiggling in his grip but too scared I'm going to hurt him further.

"And you are alive." He makes his way to an over-stuffed brocade sofa and sets me down. Just as his knee touches the floor, he hisses and presses his forehead into the cushion. "That's all that matters," he says through clenched teeth.

Manon hurries to his side, lifting his shirt to examine his side.

"He needs Ghost Pipe" Her worried expression doesn't inspire confidence.

"That's bad, right?" Every face in the room is fixed on Manon and Bastien and, as usual, no one is listening to me.

"I have that, I believe," Leelee murmurs and rushes out of the room.

Manon probes the wound, ignoring Bastian's groans until he shouts something in French and pulls away. My stomach dips seeing the wound under his shirt, and it is not pretty.

He said he doesn't bleed, and that's weirdly true, but blood isn't necessary to make this injury look dire. The edges of his skin are blackened, and the torn flesh - if you can call it that - is ragged and dull compared to what lies beneath it. When Bastien explained that the Mothers had created him from energy, he wasn't exaggerating. What would be sinew and muscle in a human is a glistening matrix of undulating, nebulous matter beneath his skin. Without meaning to, I gape at his wound, trying to make sense of it.

As I watch, the dullness spreads further, disappearing beneath the torn edges of the wound. He's trying to hide his pain, but it radiates despite his efforts.

"Do something!" I call out, though still, no one is paying attention to me.

"Try to stay still, Bastien. I'll be back." Manon rises and leaves the room in a hurry.

We're alone now, so I crawl off the couch and sit next to Bastien on the floor. He's clenching his jaw so hard I can see what should be muscles, *but is something else entirely*, working beneath his skin. I don't know why, but I place one hand on his cheek and the other on his hip, just below the wound. I'm truly grasping at straws, but maybe with this new power of mine, I can help.

My fingers tingle with the cold wave of energy I felt before, but this time I try to meter it out, rather than explode like I did before. As soon as the sensation begins, Bastien's head snaps up, and our eyes lock.

"Ah, *cher*, what are you doing?" he whispers, confusion and wonder etched across his face.

"I have no idea," I murmur as I urge more of the vibrations in my fingers to spread to him. The chill changes to warmth, thick and golden. As our energy weaves together, Bastien lifts his hand to his face, his fingers covering mine as he looks down at his side.

"*Ce qui se passe?*" His voice trembles.

I don't know what he means, but he's still staring down at his side, so I follow.

The wound is closing. White, crackling energy dances along the blackened edges, rejuvenating them and drawing them together. The tingling in my hands fades as the wound completely closes.

The world moves in slow motion. There is no room, no floor, only the magic coursing through my hands into Bastien. Our energy mingles and blends in harmony, and it becomes impossible to tell where my magic ends and his begins.

I look back at Bastien, his eyes wide with wonder.

Then he kisses me.

More than kissing, he's consuming me. As our lips touch, his energy comes alive. His arms fold me into his chest, and my hands reach for his neck, my fingers tangling in his hair. His breath is sweet, and he tastes like pure joy, each sensation on my tongue sending ripples through my body. God, I can't get close enough.

Finally, biology requires that I come up for air, but pulling away from him is the hardest thing I've ever done. I have never felt this safe before, but with that security comes a massive wave of guilt.

Seth tried so hard to protect me, but Bastien actually did.

"*Mon Dieu*," he breathes. "What are you?"

"A one-of-a-kind, powerful being that's not supposed to exist."

I scramble back from Bastien to find Leelee standing at the end of the sofa.

"Manon!" she calls out, subtle amusement evident in her eyes. The taller fae woman strides back into the room in a panic, but stops when she sees Bastien sitting up. "I think it is safe to say Bastien is going to be fine."

Manon kneels by Bastien, her jaw dropping as her hands flit along the silvery scar marking where his wound once was.

"Oh, I can't wait to study this!" she beams, turning to Leelee. "You were right."

"Right about what?" I cast a quick glance at Bastien, who looks as puzzled as I feel.

Leelee smiles, looking like a proud mother.

"Octavia, you are who completes the magic that will save us from vampires once and for all."

38

DEEP END

Octavia

HOURS PASS BEFORE LEELEE and Manon retreat from the sitting room and leave me to rest. They've been questioning me about my magic, the storm, and the vampires until I can't think anymore. I still don't know what I did or how I did it, but they seem like they have an idea. I don't have the energy to wonder about it - I'll leave it to them.

Now, all I have left in me is being pulled under by the heavy weight of not knowing what happened to Seth. All I wanted to do was go back for him. Find him. *Save him.* But he told Bastien to take me and go. He made it clear that I should stay away from him. Closing my eyes, I still see him in Illion's basement, covered in blood, and my breath catches.

That was not the Seth I know; Bastien said that Seth was gone.

They tell me it is nearly dawn outside of Briarwood. When I pull the fluffy blanket up beneath my chin, a strange little cuckoo clock I didn't notice before chimes five times, the odd sound a fitting addition to Leelee's fae cottage. She must have added it for my benefit.

I finally have a moment to myself where I'm not trying to escape death. My body is ready to sleep, but my brain has other plans. The last twenty-four hours continue to rewind again and again on a repeating loop, some portions more vivid than others.

My heart still flutters from my interaction with Bastien. My cheeks flush, and a warmth spreads in my belly. Maybe the magic has me revved up, or maybe it's him. Everything has become so convoluted now; I don't know the boundaries of my new magic when I'm with him. I can't help but feel drawn to him, and that scares me to death.

Until tonight, Bastien has been a balm for my crushing anxiety, but the pendulum is swinging in the other direction now. Would he try to influence me and make me feel something for him? It doesn't seem to fit with who he's portrayed himself to be. Tonight, he seemed to be as confused as I am.

Then my thoughts cycle to Seth again, and the pit in my stomach widens. Whatever has happened to him, I know he's still in there, and he's still fighting. That's the only reason he'd tell Bastien to take me away - I'm sure of it. But something about the way he showed no emotion bothers me. That's not my Seth. I have always been the center of his universe. His purpose and goal were to keep me safe and to build a life for us, but that look in his expressionless eyes? The way he didn't make eye contact with me? He really might not be the same anymore.

Fucking Illion.

This is his doing. For the last three years, I willingly endured absolute torture because we thought it would keep me safe. I did it for myself, yes, but I also did it for Seth. And after everything, it turns out Illion is a snake, lying to both of us just so he could secretly suppress who I really am. Or not. I still don't know the truth about my childhood. Either way, whatever he was doing to me wasn't good. My soul shatters, my eyes burning as I pull the covers over my head. There's no telling what he's done to Seth, but the possibilities make my stomach turn.

I wriggle down into piles of pillows on the sofa and try closing my eyes, but sleep still refuses to come.

A crunching noise makes me jump, and I push up on my elbows.

I peer over the side of the sofa to see Bastien standing outside the door. My heart flutters.

He's not touching me, so he's not infusing me with his magical feel-good juju right now, but there is no denying that my body and my heart remember.

"Ah, *mon cœur*," he whispers, "*ça va?*"

I sit back on the pillows and cross my arms. So much for trying to clear my head. When he speaks like that, my brain stops working.

"I don't speak French," I mumble, trying my best to sound unaffected.

"*Cajun* French, *cher*." I can hear the smile in his voice, and it is maddeningly sweet. Soft footsteps pad in time with my heart, then he's standing beside me.

"What I asked you was... how..." he says, settling on the edge of the couch and leaning over me.

Damn him.

"Are..." His mouth hovers over mine. I don't dare even breathe.

"You?" The corner of his mouth turns up in a little smirk. I'm captivated, unable to tear my eyes away from the subtle curve of his lips. He lifts my chin, placing the softest kiss on my forehead.

I exhale and drop my eyes, too embarrassed to look at him. He has me hook, line, and sinker. There's no evidence he's trying to influence me magically, but the way he's moving and talking and, well, being - that's a different story.

"You are confusing me," I finally say.

He touches my hair, tucks it behind my ear, and leaves his hand on my cheek, his thumb tracing the skin just beneath my eye.

"No, *cher,* I'm protecting you."

39

I'M GOING OUT OF MY MIND

Seth

JESUS, IT HURTS!

I close my eyes and gulp down shaky breaths after bolting the door to the shed. The pain is unbearable, my body trembling uncontrollably from the shock. Blisters cover my hands, my face, my chest, and they are already beginning to open and weep.

I console myself with the knowledge that they will heal as I shed the wet clothing clinging to my lower body. I cast my eyes around hoping for a scrap of anything to wipe the water from my skin, but I am out of luck. It's a common theme for me right now.

Water drips from the ceiling in so many places it's impossible to escape, stinging me wherever it hits. I look for the driest corner and slide down to the floor while the wind howls around the run-down shack I stumbled on in the middle of the piney woods. The dilapidated structure might look like Illion's, but this is too far away to have any connection to him. I ran as long as I could while my skin screamed and my heart tore itself in two.

I think I heard noises following me, so I don't believe I am in the clear. They'll find me, I am sure of it, but for now I am free.

It was so much harder than I thought it would be - letting Octavia go. I would have given anything to have held her again, but that wasn't possible. I know what she is - my mother's project to end my father's reign - and I didn't intend to fall in love with her. But I did - a secret I managed to keep from everyone. At least. I thought I had.

I did everything right. I played the part Mother asked of me. However, from day one, when I carried her unconscious body out of the research lab and felt the low, steady hum of her magic trying to resurface, I was a lost cause. She was an angel, an impossible, exquisite fae and vampire goddess entrusted to my care and, in that moment, I swore to protect her.

Look at me now.

I can't stop seeing her in the arms of the Kretarie. It broke me. I left the shattered pieces of my heart back there on the road, and as much as I want nothing more than to hold her again, there's no way in hell I can be near her now - not after what Illion has done to me.

The first part was hard enough - killing innocent, captive humans.

But now? If I'm not within Illion's reach, I pray I can wait out whatever he has done to me, that it will fade. I can only hope that, in time, I will become myself again.

Because if feeding on fae is the only way for me to survive, I'd rather die tonight.

ACKNOWLEDGMENTS

In 2021, I was a part of a consortium of writers who were feeling their way through the indie publishing world. Covid was winding down, the world was waking back up, and we had the crazy idea of putting together an anthology of short stories—short stories about vampires.

The anthology never happened, but before its untimely demise, I sat down and began a story about vampires that felt a little like Damon and Stephan, but with new and unusual problems. Forget daylight rings or vervain, these vampires of mine would be hurt by water and could only drink A negative blood. Why? I have no idea.

So, thank you Karen Hough for the vampire anthology idea that led to Let It Rain, and thank you Kindle Vella for the brief existence that saw me complete the first draft of this story.

Mom, you amaze me with your willingness to read and reread my books and your undying love of vampire stories. Spike, Damon, and Angel would be proud.

A great big thank you goes to my editor, Casey, who is solely responsible for naming the Kretarie. And who would have thought that a friendship struck up on TikTok would lead to this level of collaboration? I am so glad the universe tossed us in the same space and I will forever ask myself what my characters are thinking, thanks to you.

Thank you to all my friends and family who put up with my rambling about these crazy stories I tell. Your support makes this writing endeavor doable. Thank you Scott for being willing to read whatever I write and lastly, thank you to my readers. I am so glad to have shared a little piece of my imagination with you. I hope you enjoyed reading it as much as I did writing it.

THE MUSIC

WHEN I STARTED WRITING Let It Rain, I began adding
song titles as chapter names. Artistically, I have been a
musician most of my life, and music has an enormous
amount of impact and meaning for me, especially when I
write. But what started out as a quirky, fun addition to the
story became a mission. Some of these songs were chosen
for the meaning of the words. Others made the list for the
lyrics or the music itself. A few have it all. So I have created
a Spotify playlist with these songs, in chapter order, if
you ever want to get inside my head (or the character's
heads) just a little more. I've added the song list below that
explains why I chose each one. The name of the playlist
and the Spotify link are at the end. Enjoy!

1. *Oops!... I Did It Again – Britney Spears*: Just a girl
   wanting some Oreos and risking her life to do it.

2. *Hold Your Breath - Astyria:* I felt the darkness in
   this song aligned with the gravity of the situation.

The lyrics, percussion, and bass, especially.

3. *The Chemicals Between Us - Bush:* I mean, it's Bush. Not much more to say. The title fits like a glove, too.

4. *Bad Habits - Ed Sheeran:* The title itself fits, but the lyrics connect for me, too.

5. *Is It Over Now? - Taylor Swift:* Great song, but this is mostly about the title.

6. I*t's In My Blood – ANA X, T.H.O.R., Sybrid, Kat Meoz:* Another perfect title fit, but the darkness of the music is also spot on.

7. *Land of Confusion - Phil Collins (Cover by Hidden Citizens):* The title is everything and the song just hits (and has since the 80's).

8. *One Wrong Move – Power-Haus, Klergy, Lloren*: This song has the mood of this moment. A little sinister, a little dark, and it hits with the idea that one wrong move can make all the difference between life an death.

9. *Mother, Mother - Tracy Bonham:* Once upon a time, I covered this song in my band. I always loved this song. It's sweet, mean, and angry all

rolled into one which embodies Genevive Dormande one hundred percent.

10. *Running With The Wolves - Aurora-* This song has such a presence, but I mostly included it for the title. It is included on many of my writing playlists, though.

11. *Policy of Truth - Depeche Mode:* Paying the price, subterfuge, nefarious dealings... the whole thing just fits.

12. *Run to the Hills - Klara Hammarstrom:* Not the one you thought it was, hmmm? This sounded like Octavia.

13. *Trouble - Valerie Broussard:* The perfect song to take us into the bayou. This one has been on my writing playlist for *Let It Rain* since the beginning.

14. *The Patron Saint of Liars and Fakes - Fall Out Boy:* It's Illion. Need I say more?

15. *Do You Believe in Magic? - The Lovin Spoonful (Cover by Bien):* Definitely picked for the title, though this version fits more than the original, I think.

16. *Hold My Hand - Lady Gaga:* The Bastien Effect.

17. *Landmines - BELLSAINT:* One of my favorite songs ever. It is the most perfectly tragic song and it is a glimpse into Seth's broken body and mind.

18. *People Are Strange - The Doors (Cover by Echo & the Bunnymen):* Another perfect fit, but this time it's the Mothers.

19. *Astronomical - SVRCINA:* the last song added (because this was the last chapter I wrote). I needed to capture Bastien's fascination and need beginning to blossom.

20. *Waking Up - MJ Cole and Freya Ridings:* I heard this on the TV show, A Discovery of Witches and just knew. The title is perfect, but the music really fits the magic and mystery in this chapter.

21. *Even If It Hurts - Sam Tinne:* This song captures the inner resolve that Genevive has when she has to confront Arthur.

22. *Here Come the Monsters - ADONA:* This chapter marks the real spiral down for Seth. It's getting super-real for him here and the lyrics as well as the tone reflect this chapter's mood.

23. *Torn - Natalie Imbruglia*: Another throwback. Tavi is starting to feel the tug of Bastien. This song is more about the title, but some of the lyrics are applicable.

24. *Figure You Out - Voila*: This should be the theme song for the whole book. We are getting into Bastien's head and it is delicious.

25. *You Gotta Run - Kergy and Ames*: Here we go. Tavi is on the run now. This sing started as a title-only association, but the more I listened to it, the more it seemed to fit.

26. *Zero Gravity – of Verona*: Such a bittersweet song. It came on just as the idea to insert a Bastien chapter formed at the eleventh hour. I was Team Bastien from the get-go, but then I flipped back to Seth, but this little glimpse into Bastien tugged at my heart and now I am completely and utterly torn.

27. *Brave New World - Kalandra*: Enter the wonder of the Wilds. Tavi finds that her world isn't what it seems and this song and title really seemed to speak to the mood of the fae and the Wilds.

28. *The Story of My Life - One Direction*: Melancholy

and bittersweet, just like all the new information
Tavi is receiving. Title and song both apply here.

29. *Behind the Mask - Ivy & Gold*: This song touches
on so many things – Illion's lies, Genevive's love,
and all the entanglements that come with being
Seth.

30. *Heaven Help Me - Raign*: Title, music, lyrics – it's
all there. Poor Bastien. He wants to what is right,
but conflict is etched in everything he touches
now.

31. *Tomorrow Waits - Klergy and Mindy Jones*: This
song has a title that caught my attention and
of course, the song itself resonated, too. Tavi is
preparing for her rescue, not really knowing what
will happen.

32. *Taste - Stray Kids*: The mystery and darkness in
this song felt right. The title also hits because of
what is going on with Seth. It smacks of desire,
which mirrors the conflict in his situation – desire
for Tavi versus the desire for other blood being
instilled in him artificially.

33. *Escape - Stray Kids*: A favorite of mine, but the
lyrics don't quite fit. The title and the mood,

though? Absolutely.

34. *How To Save a Life - The Fray*: This whole song is a mood. Tavi wants to save him. She is desperate to get Seth out of danger, but it begins to feel futile and her heart is breaking and remaking because of it.

35. *Wrecking Ball - Miley Cyrus*: I mean, you get it right? These lyrics are surprisingly fitting and you can apply them in so many different ways. Is it about Seth? Bastien? Her whole damn life? There is no wrong answer.

36. *Ready for War - Tommee Profitt and Liv Ash*: The title, and the song, speaks for itself.

37. *Oh My, My - Ruelle*: This is a whole song addition. There's a new energy brewing as Tavi finds her magic and the pull of Bastien sets in.

38. *Deep End - Ruelle*: Another whole song application. Mystery, connection, loss, magic...

39. *I'm Going Out of My Mind - Lawless and MXMS*: This one HURTS. I have difficulty even listening to it sometimes, and the wounding nature hits as hard as Seth's new reality.

Let it Rain Chapters

on Spotify

https://open.spotify.com/playlist/2riaO14JHhce4zGW
WeCdHg?si=ea6e432a940a4c63

ABOUT THE AUTHOR

ESCAPISM IS HER DRUG of choice. As a child, she was angry that her existence was confined to this reality, and she did everything she could to find a way out. Stories made it bearable. Whether it was Thor's Bifrost, Narnia's wardrobe, or the mirror in Stephen R. Donaldson's *Mordant's Need* duology, she was hooked. Now, she tells her own stories of escape. She creates and invites others to find solace, adventure, love, and passion in fantasy realms, outer space, and reinvented parallel realities. This door is always open.

B.G. Vandenberg has always written stories. She works as a middle school science instructional coach in Texas and has three grown children, a loving partner, her dog named Scout, and three exceptionally unusual cats.

She can be found at:
https://www.thebookishberg.com
FB: B.G. Vandenberg, Author
TT: @bgvandenbergauthor
IG: @bgvandenbergauthor